"Can I see Ruby?"

"I don't think that's wise." Stella's voice was firm.

"Is it illegal?"

"Because you retained the right to contact, not really, but it's highly unusual. There are no procedures for allowing that contact when there are no parents...."

"But that doesn't mean I can't see her."

Stella leaned forward again, her eyes deadly serious. "Rachel, please, don't do this to yourself. There's nothing to be gained."

A little girl, not even two years old, was being shuffled around like a sack of dirty laundry. Five homes. In less than two years she'd have bonded with five different families.

Unless her young survival instincts kicked in and she quit bonding altogether.

Rachel turned cold. And then hot. She started to shake. The world was dark everywhere except for the pinpoint where Stella's face remained.

"I don't just want to see her," she whispered. "I want to take her. Home. To live with me."

D0051394

Dear Reader,

Welcome back to Trueblood! I know you've already met town residents Rachel Blair and Max Santana. They're engaged to be married, and their wedding day has arrived, but Rachel, it seems, has some painful secrets that she's been keeping from all of us. As you learn about them, I hope you'll receive her with the warmth and compassion she so desperately needs. She's a good person, a strong woman whose motivation has always been to do what's right. To do what's best for those around her in spite of the personal cost to herself. Rachel has learned some interesting things about serving others as she traveled this journey, and they were things that I think I needed to learn, as well. We're only as good to others as we are good for ourselves. We can't tend to others unless we tend to ourselves. So while self-sacrifice is most often viewed as a good thing, it can also be, ultimately, the worst choice we can make. I invite you to read on. Join Rachel and Max as their story unfolds, and let me know what you think....

I can be reached at ttquinn@home.com

Tara

TRUEBLOOD, TEXAS

Tara Taylor Quinn

The Rancher's Bride

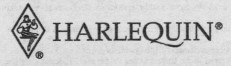

HARLEQUIN®

TORONTO • NEW YORK • LONDON
AMSTERDAM • PARIS • SYDNEY • HAMBURG
STOCKHOLM • ATHENS • TOKYO • MILAN • MADRID
PRAGUE • WARSAW • BUDAPEST • AUCKLAND

Tara Taylor Quinn is acknowledged
as the author of this work.

For my father, Walter Wright Gumser, Mr. 9/23/24,
who, no matter what, loved me unconditionally—
a gift that transcends every earthly thing.

HARLEQUIN BOOKS
225 Duncan Mill Road, Don Mills,
Ontario, Canada M3B 3K9

ISBN 0-373-65088-4

THE RANCHER'S BRIDE

TRUEBLOOD, TEXAS

THE TRUEBLOOD LEGACY

THE YEAR WAS 1918, and the Great War in Europe still raged, but Esau Porter was heading home to Texas.

The young sergeant arrived at his parents' ranch northwest of San Antonio on a Sunday night, only the celebration didn't go off as planned. Most of the townsfolk of Carmelita had come out to welcome Esau home, but when they saw the sorry condition of the boy, they gave their respects quickly and left.

The fever got so bad so fast that Mrs. Porter hardly knew what to do. By Monday night, before the doctor from San Antonio made it into town, Esau was dead.

The Porter family grieved. How could their son have survived the German peril, only to burn up and die in his own bed? It wasn't much of a surprise when Mrs. Porter took to her bed on Wednesday. But it was a hell of a shock when half the residents of Carmelita came down with the horrible illness. House after house was hit by death, and all the townspeople could do was pray for salvation.

None came. By the end of the year, over one hundred souls had perished. The influenza virus took those in the prime of life, leaving behind an unprecedented number of orphans. And the virus knew no boundaries. By the time the threat had passed, more than thirty-seven million people had succumbed worldwide.

But in one house, there was still hope.

Isabella Trueblood had come to Carmelita in the late 1800s with her father, blacksmith Saul Trueblood, and her mother, Teresa Collier Trueblood. The family had traveled from Indiana, leaving their Quaker roots behind.

Young Isabella grew up to be an intelligent woman who had a gift for healing and storytelling. Her dreams centered on the boy next door, Foster Carter, the son of Chester and Grace.

Just before the bad times came in 1918, Foster asked Isabella to be his wife, and the future of the Carter spread was secured. It was a happy union, and the future looked bright for the young couple.

Two years later, not one of their relatives was alive. How the young couple had survived was a miracle. And during the epidemic, Isabella and Foster had taken in more than twenty-two orphaned children from all over the county. They fed them, clothed them, taught them as if they were blood kin.

Then Isabella became pregnant, but there were complications. Love for her handsome son, Josiah, born in 1920, wasn't enough to stop her from growing weaker by the day. Knowing she couldn't leave her husband to tend to all the children if she died, she set out to find families for each one of her orphaned charges.

And so the Trueblood Foundation was born. Named in memory of Isabella's parents, it would become famous all over Texas. Some of the orphaned children went to strangers, but many were reunited with their families. After reading notices in newspapers and church bulletins, aunts, uncles, cousins and grandparents rushed to Carmelita to find the young ones they'd given up for dead.

Toward the end of Isabella's life, she'd brought together more than thirty families, and not just her orphans. Many others, old and young, made their way to her doorstep, and Isabella turned no one away.

At her death, the town's name was changed to Trueblood, in her honor. For years to come, her simple grave was adorned with flowers on the anniversary of her death, grateful tokens of appreciation from the families she had brought together.

Isabella's son, Josiah, grew into a fine rancher and married Rebecca Montgomery in 1938. They had a daughter, Elizabeth Trueblood Carter, in 1940. Elizabeth married her neighbor William Garrett in 1965, and gave birth to twins Lily and Dylan in 1971, and daughter Ashley a few years later. Home was the Double G ranch, about ten miles from Trueblood proper, and the Garrett children grew up listening to stories of their famous great-grandmother, Isabella. Because they were Truebloods, they knew that they, too, had a sacred duty to carry on the tradition passed down to them: finding lost souls and reuniting loved ones.

CHAPTER ONE

OH, GOD. She wasn't going to be able to do it.

Her wedding day had finally arrived. The day she was to marry Max Santana. Though for years he'd done nothing more than humor her, she'd been in love with the man since puberty. Her wildest dream, her most fantastic hope was about to come true.

And she couldn't do it.

Hands shaking, Rachel Blair reached up to unhook the lacy white veil from her hair. Her father, the Reverend Donald Blair, was going over the last-minute details outside on the acre of green lawn in back of the First Trueblood Presbyterian Church, where he was scheduled, in less than an hour, to perform the ceremony for the wedding of his only daughter. Guests would be arriving soon. As would Max. If he hadn't already.

Rachel's long red hair tumbled around her shoulders and down her back as she removed the pins the hairdresser had put in earlier that morning. Even that little freedom was a relief. And an ache.

She wanted, more than anything else in life, to marry Max. To live side by side with him, share the aches and joys of daily life, to eat with him every day and sleep with him every night...

The hairpins hardly made a sound as they slipped from Rachel's fingers to the tile floor of the choir changing room, which was serving double duty as the bride's dressing room this Saturday morning.

Jumping up from her stool, Rachel glanced around frantically. She had to get changed, get out of here, before it was too late. Before anyone came in and tried to stop her. Ashley Garrett Blackstone, the youngest daughter of the Trueblood Garretts, was already a couple of minutes late and would be running in any moment in typical Ashley fashion, strong, sure, ready to go. Pregnancy hadn't changed her a bit. And with her take-charge friend there, Rachel wouldn't stand a chance.

With their goals scattering them in different directions, Rachel and Ashley hadn't seen each other all that much since leaving Trueblood for college. Rachel, hankering for home, had settled in at the Isabella Trueblood Memorial Library, after a brief stint as a librarian in San Antonio. Ashley lived in a high-rise in the heart of San Antonio and worked as an account executive at a top advertising firm. She knew nothing about the year that had changed Rachel's life.

And Rachel couldn't seem to tell her. Couldn't bring herself to tell anyone. Not even Max.

Only her father knew the truth. But it wasn't something they talked about. That long, debilitating year of Rachel's life was still too painful for both of them.

Her father. He'd had such hopes for today. Hopes for her. And her future. Hopes that she'd finally be happy, truly happy, again.

She had to get out. Get away.

Hearing a car door and Ashley's voice outside the window, Rachel picked up the folds of her wedding gown and ran through the connecting door to the choir loft at the front of the deserted sanctuary, past the silent pulpit, down through the rows of pews and out the side door of the church. Until the guests started arriving and walking back to the rows of chairs set up on the lawn, the side parking lot would be empty. Thankfully, blissfully, sadly empty.

Running was a little difficult in her spike-heeled wedding shoes—the ones the saleslady in San Antonio had insisted would make her calves looked sinfully sexy to her new husband when he helped her out of her wedding dress later that night.

Kicking them off, Rachel barely felt the sting of the stones beneath her feet as she headed for the parsonage, the building that had been home to her the majority of her life. Her suitcase and purse were there, all packed and ready for the honeymoon. They had everything she'd need. Essentials, credit card, cash. And some things she wouldn't—like the negligees she was terrified to wear.

Damn Neil Harris and his groping hands, his superior strength. Tears streamed down Rachel's face, almost unnoticed, as she slipped into her father's house, grabbed her things and ran out again.

And damn her own naive stupidity. And her recklessness. She was to blame for everything that had happened. She knew that. Had always known, even though her father had never once pointed the finger of blame in her direction.

She was to blame, and somehow she was going to have to find a way to come to terms with the events that had taken place that fateful night in Austin, in a car not far from the University of Texas. And everything that had happened afterward as well. The choices she'd made. The things she'd done.

She'd thought she was over it all. Beyond it as much

as she ever would be. At least enough to get on with the rest of her life.

She'd thought she'd recovered. Right up until she came face-to-face with her wedding night.

She just couldn't do it.

With one last, tearful glance back, Rachel disappeared into the warm May sunshine, leaving her beloved groom standing at the makeshift altar, the solid gold band they'd chosen together nestled in his pocket.

NEVER ONE to socialize much, thirty-five-year-old Max Santana shifted his weight restlessly from one foot to the next, waiting for Reverend Blair to give the signal for "The Wedding March" to start. The anticipatory trill emanating from the crowd of well-wishers seated in the white folding chairs before him fed his restlessness.

Only for Rachel would he go through this. For his green-eyed, red-haired temptress he'd do anything.

Dylan Garrett, five years Max's junior and the closest thing to a brother Max had ever had, leaned over.

"You doing okay?" he asked gruffly.

Dylan looked a lot more at ease in the black tux he was wearing than Max felt in the one that was choking him.

"Fine." It was a piece of cake. Or would be. Just as soon as Rachel got her butt out of that church and up the aisle beside him. Nine months was a long time for a man to wait once he'd finally figured out where his future led.

Old-fashioned enough to want to do things right—and with the Reverend Donald Blair as his future father-in-law—Max had been forced to take some mighty cold showers this past winter. But all that would soon be over. Tonight, he was going to have Rachel right where she belonged. In his bed.

She'd be lucky if he let her up before their first anniversary. No man had ever had to put up with as much tempting as Rachel had thrown his way. Hell, she'd been trying out her feminine wiles on him for most of ten years. From the time she'd turned fourteen and decided she was officially a woman.

Heaven help him.

He'd managed to ignore her, for the most part, until that first day she'd come home from college. By God, he'd noticed her then.

And she'd made certain he kept right on noticing.

Or had she? Maybe she hadn't been as much the temptress these last months. But her big green eyes had still shone with that same adoration they'd always had.

She'd grown up at the university. And while he loved her more than any man should ever love a woman, Max was a little saddened by the pixie that had been lost in the transition.

He glanced at his watch. "The Wedding March" was supposed to have started two minutes ago.

Max continued to rock. And took a second to look out over the sea of people facing him. William Garrett. William's daughter Lily and her husband Cole and their new baby. Teachers he'd had in school. Ranch hands. Boots. A woman or two he'd bedded along the way. Friends of the Garrett family. Associates from the feed store. Mike from the gas station. Familiar faces, all of them, he thought, warmed by their support. He might not be a Garrett in any official capacity, but he'd grown up with them, attended every holiday, every family celebration as though he were one of them. And today, he was being treated as well as any Garrett.

Everyone in Trueblood had turned out for his wedding to Rachel Blair.

Even Sebastian Cooper had come down for the event. Max had a bad feeling about the man, but he'd been one of Dylan's best friends for years so Max tried to tolerate him. Unlike a good whiskey, the man definitely did not improve with age.

"You think Cole'll be able to oversee the horses?" Max asked Dylan under his breath.

Dylan's rangy brother-in-law was going to fill in as ranch foreman while Max was away. Cole and Dylan's twin sister, Lily, had a small spread attached to the Garrett ranch.

"I'm sure of it," Dillon said sotto voce. "He ran his own ranch before marrying Lily, remember. And Dad'll be there."

"Humph." Max didn't like to see the elderly Garrett out working the ranch. That was Max's job, so William, who'd put in his time and then some, could sit back and enjoy life.

And maybe find himself a good woman.

"Cole's a dad now, and he's got his own place to see to," Max said, his hands clenched behind his back. Where in the hell was Rachel?

Why wasn't Reverend Blair out there, giving the signal? First Presbyterian's organist had been sending covert glances in the direction of the church for several minutes.

And the crowd was getting restless. They reminded Max of a herd of calves at branding time. Overly excited. And getting more nervous by the minute.

"Fatherhood is only spurring Cole on, not deterring him from his work," Dylan said through the side of his mouth.

It took Max a second to figure out what his friend was even talking about.

Tempted to yank at the bow tie clipped around his neck, Max ran through a mental calculation of the hands he'd left in charge of the ranch, instead. He didn't spend a lot of time talking with them, but they were honest card players. And hard workers. They could handle things for a week so William wouldn't have to.

He was finding it increasingly hard to breathe.

Max brushed his arm against the inside pocket of his jacket, reassured by the jeweler's box he'd placed there. Traditionally, Dylan should be holding the ring, but Max had wanted to keep it himself. It somehow made him feel more in control of his own destiny.

Rachel was ten minutes late.

People were starting to talk a little louder, to turn around. He'd even seen one or two of them send veiled glances his way.

What? Did they think Rachel would walk out on him? Everyone knew she'd been in love with him for almost half her life.

Of course, most of those years had been nothing more than puppy love. A crush. But still…

Did they honestly think she wouldn't go through with the marriage?

Max started to sweat. Could he blame her if she got cold feet? He was almost twelve years older than her. A big, rugged outdoorsman. A ranch foreman. What would a slight, innocent minister's daughter see in him?

"She probably ripped her dress or cried off her makeup," Dylan said, speaking a little louder than before to be heard over the crowd of well-wishers who were simultaneously mingling in conversation with those seated close by and watching the back of the churchyard where Reverend Blair was due to put in his appearance.

Feet sweating in his shoes, Max wished for the cowboy boots and jeans he was at home in. He could tell Dylan was getting a little worried, too.

Max should never have asked her to marry him—a woman so much younger than him. Hell, she'd been in second grade when he was a senior in high school.

To think that a quiet set-in-his-ways rancher like him would really attract a young woman like Rachel for life…

What was he thinking? Of course Rachel loved him. He might have a hang-up about their age difference, but she certainly didn't.

"There…"

Max's head shot up as Dylan whispered the word. Reverend Blair had appeared at the back of the rows of chairs and was signaling—but not to the organist. He wanted Max. And his face was lined with worry.

Alarm shooting through his veins, Max made it back to his future father-in-law without even seeing the rows of friends and family sitting there watching him. What they were thinking was unimportant. Something was wrong with Rachel.

"Is she sick?" he asked urgently, before the good reverend could get out the first word. "Where is she?"

Reverend Blair shook his head. "I'm sorry, son.…" He backed into the open door of the church, away from prying eyes.

"Sorry about what?" Max asked, no less urgently, following Donald Blair step for step. Whatever it was, he'd take care of it.

"She's gone...."

"Gone where?" Dear God, don't let him say she was dead. Anything but dead. Dead he couldn't do anything about. "How?"

Had there been an accident?

The minister shrugged his slumped shoulders and Max had the distinct feeling that the other man knew more than he intended to tell Max.

"She ran off, Max."

Max swung around, seeing Ashley Garrett Blackstone for the first time. Dylan's youngest sister had been standing in the shadows. She was supposed to be attending Rachel.

Who'd gone.

"Ran off?" he asked, frowning. This entire day was going from uncomfortable to nightmarish. "Where? With whom?"

This wasn't like Rachel at all. Rachel Blair always did what was expected of her. She was the town librarian, for God's sake. He glanced back at the reverend.

Donald Blair's eyes were filled with an unsettling combination of worry and sadness. "Her suitcase and purse are gone from the house."

"We found these in the yard between the church and the parsonage," Ashley said, holding up a pair of white high heels. "They were Rachel's wedding shoes."

"Someone's kidnapped her? She's been abducted?" Max hollered. "Why are you all just standing here? Call the police."

The reverend shook his head. "I already called," he said. "They don't take missing person reports for forty-eight hours. It would have been pretty hard for someone to take her from the choir changing room, which is where I left her," he continued. "And even if they had, I doubt they'd have stopped by the parsonage for her suitcase and purse. And only her suitcase and purse. In the first place, they wouldn't have known they were there."

"She ran off, Max," Ashley said again, her voice gentle. Ashley's new husband was out there someplace, in that sea of people.

And so was everyone else he knew.

Max hardly cared. Rachel was all that mattered.

"Why?" he asked, hands in the pockets of his slacks as he tried to make sense of the past twenty minutes. "How long ago did she leave? Did she take the car? Leave a note?"

"Her car's at my place," Ashley said. "She came into San Antonio this morning to have her hair done and was leaving her car to be serviced while you guys were on your honeymoon. I drove her back to Trueblood. I'd just run out to the ranch to pick up the dress Lily had shortened for me and when I came back she was gone."

"There was no note," Reverend Blair added. "It looks as though she left in a bit of a hurry."

"Why?" Max asked again. And what did he do next? He knew ranching, not women.

Again the other two shrugged. "She was a bit edgy this morning, but that's natural under the circumstances," Ashley said. Max felt the first stab of real pain as he saw the compassion in her eyes. "She was also undeniably excited. She wanted to be your wife, Max."

"She did," the reverend confirmed.

"More than anything." Ashley's slim fingers ran

down the sleeve of Max's jacket. Frozen beneath her touch, he hardly felt her at all.

His glance rested on Donald Blair. "You don't seem all that surprised."

The minister looked from Max to Ashley, and then away. "I'm surprised," he said quietly. "My daughter wants to be your wife more than anything else in life."

"But?"

The minister shook his head, eyes sad with defeat. "I can't say anything more. Whatever might be bothering Rachel is between you and her."

If Max had been a loud, stomping man, he'd have been tempted to rip the reverend limb from limb until he told him whatever it was he was keeping from him. He contented himself with a nod, instead.

"Do you know where I might start looking for her?" he asked quietly.

Reverend Blair shook his head again, his eyes steadfast as they met Max's. "No, son. I have no idea. I wish I did."

"Talk to Dylan," Ashley whispered.

Max nodded again. He might not be a people finder, but his best man was. Dylan, with his sister Lily, owned Finders Keepers, an agency that specialized in locating missing family members.

Rachel might not be family yet, in a legal sense, but she was the closest family he had. He had to find her.

Something must be horribly wrong to have made her run off like she did—something that was so terrible, or frightening, that she couldn't even talk to him first. He had to know what that something was. To find a way to help her. Didn't she know that was what love was all about? Being there for each other through the worst of times?

Heading out to tell their guests—to whom Dylan was attending—that his fiancée wasn't going to make their wedding that day, Max wondered if he'd be able to wait to let Lily and Dylan do their stuff.

He had to find Rachel now.

CHAPTER TWO

"So where do we start?"

Max sat, elbows on his denim-clad knees, on the edge of the comfortable sofa in the waiting room of Finders Keepers. Located on the second floor of the Double G ranch house, Dylan and Lily's business was blessedly convenient. And the waiting room less threatening to Max than either of their offices. He wasn't really a client. Wasn't really in need of their services. This would all make perfect sense in the morning.

"With you and Reverend Blair," Lily said, seated across from him, still in her wedding finery. Her long black hair had come loose from the band she'd looped it back with and cascaded around her cheeks. Her green eyes weren't dancing the way they had been since she'd had little Elizabeth.

Dylan leaned forward. Like Max, he'd changed into jeans, too, and his sun-streaked light-brown hair looked like it needed a comb even more than usual. There was no sign on his somber face of that dimple he'd always hated being teased about.

"We need to know everything that's happened recently," Dylan said. Both he and Lily had notepads on their laps and sympathy in their eyes.

Max looked away. "She was just planning the wedding," he said. "Ashley probably knows more about that than I do."

"Yeah, we're planning to talk to Ashley, too," Lily said. "She's waiting downstairs for us."

Max looked up. "Is Reverend Blair down there, too?"

Dylan nodded.

Max could just imagine what it looked like down there in the great room. If he cared to look over the balcony. Judging by the cars he'd seen outside, the place was swarming with people—all concerned about him. Which is why he'd come in through the seldom used private entrance up to Finders Keepers. The thought of walking through that room made him sweat.

They were all staying out of his way—giving him space. For which he was eternally grateful. This would be solved soon, and then he wouldn't be suffocating under all the sympathy.

Max was the caretaker, not the one needing care. It wasn't his role. He didn't know how to play it. People needed him, not the other way around.

"So—" Lily looked down at her notepad "—has there been anything, you know, different between you and Rachel lately?"

"No."

Dylan looked him in the eye. "No arguments?"

Max stared back. "No."

"Anything she wanted that you wouldn't give her?"

He didn't even have to think about it. "No."

"Rachel's not like that, anyway," Lily said. "She'd never run off because she didn't get her way."

"Something made her go," Dylan observed.

"Did she seem upset about anything?" Lily asked. "Get any mail that you know about? Talk about old college friends?"

Max shook his head. She'd been excited about the wedding.

Or so he'd thought.

"Any changes at all?" Dylan asked. "Come on, Max, you gotta help us out a little bit here."

Standing, Max moved to stare out one of the big windows William Garrett had had installed in the back of the house. It looked out over the huge expanse of land he tended. The land he knew and understood. "The only change in Rachel was when she came back from college last year."

"What kind of change?" There was a new urgency in Dylan's voice.

Max shrugged. "Nothing to build a case on," he said. "She'd grown up, that's all. You've been working with her down at the library, Dylan—both in San Antonio and Trueblood. You must have noticed."

He saw Dylan nod in the reflection in the window.

"I personally think it was more than just growing up," Lily said. "She's never said anything, but I'm certain that she was hurt pretty badly while she was in Austin."

"Which is a normal part of growing up," Dylan countered.

"Maybe..." Lily paused.

Max didn't turn around. He couldn't. Somewhere out there his beloved was having a problem and he was trapped here, unable to do one damn thing to help her.

"I think it was more than just the normal hurts of growing up, though," Lily finished. "I think some guy must have really done a number on her."

Max had never thought of that. He probably should have.

Cold terror struck his heart. Was it possible that Rachel didn't love him? That she loved another man? Someone he knew nothing about? Someone younger? Someone she'd run to rather than tie herself to a lifetime as a rancher's wife?

"I wonder if she's being threatened," Lily said. "Or blackmailed."

Max blanched. He hadn't thought of that, either.

"I doubt it," Dylan replied. "I suppose it's possible, but that's a bit of a stretch." Max saw him turn, look toward the window where Max was standing. "She didn't say anything to you about yearnings or goals, like a position with a bigger library—or something outside the library altogether?" he asked. "Or maybe wanting to live in the city someday?"

"Something that would make marriage to the foreman of the Double G not an appealing prospect, you mean?" Max summed up. He *had* thought of that.

"Not…"

"It's okay," Max said, cutting him off. "It's a possibility, but no, she's given no indication of anything of the sort. She'd always told me she never wanted to live anywhere but right here in Trueblood."

So why'd she leave? The question filled the sudden silence.

"Could be she was running from whatever, or whoever, hurt her at the university…." Lily's voice trailed off.

And then, when both men remained silent, she continued. "It's not like her to not leave a note. If she just wanted to call off the wedding and was afraid to tell Max for some reason, maybe afraid to hurt him, she'd still have been conscientious enough to leave a note for him. And for her father, too. This isn't like Rachel at all."

Max felt like he had a rock where his gut used to be.

"Okay." Dylan stood. Though not as tall as Max, his muscular six-foot-one-inch frame was still impressive. "If you're sure there's nothing more you can give us, we need to speak with the others."

Max nodded, knew he needed to leave, but was unusually reluctant to return to the solitude of his cabin. That was a first.

"So what happens next?" he asked.

Dylan joined him by the window. Max could hear Lily heading down the stairs, probably to get their next interviewee.

"We've already checked at Carmelita's Diner, Isabella's Bar, and the motel. We know she isn't in town. So we talk to everyone else downstairs, hopefully come up with something a little more substantial to go on."

"And if you don't?" Max continued to stare out the window. The stark vastness was somehow reassuring to him. It was familiar.

"Then we start tracing credit cards, bank account action, airlines, bus stations in San Antonio, keep asking around town to see if we can find anyone who knows what direction she went...."

"Everyone in town was sitting in the backyard of the church."

"Someone may have seen something," Dylan said. "And then," he added softly, "we wait."

That sounded like a death sentence.

"Check your messages when you get home," he continued. "She may have called."

He'd already checked. Three times. There'd been nothing.

Max clenched his jaw against the sudden stab of pain. "This isn't like her."

Dylan was close enough that Max could feel the other man's heat. "I know."

"How sure are you that she wasn't abducted?"

"Ninety-nine percent."

Both men turned as footsteps pounded up the stairs. William Garrett appeared, slightly out of breath. "Someone just called from down at Isabella's. Apparently they were talking down there about the, uh, day and some cowhand passing through said he saw a woman in a wedding dress hopping into a pickup truck out on FM 1022 about two hours ago. They were heading toward San Antonio."

Max's throat closed up.

Moments later, the phone rang. Lily spoke quietly with the caller, and then hung up. She glanced at Max and then away. "Rachel's car is gone."

MAX, ALWAYS PREPARED, threw a change of clothes and a toothbrush into a leather satchel, grabbed the keys to his truck and pulled the front door of his cabin shut behind him two minutes after he'd arrived back home. He couldn't just sit there and wait. He had to do something.

Even if that something meant combing the streets of San Antonio one by one looking for Rachel's car.

If she didn't love him, if she'd left just because of him, he'd deal with that when he found her. For now, he believed she was having some kind of problem and he wasn't going to rest until he knew whether or not he could help her. Until he'd done whatever he could to make things right again.

Passing the ranch house on his way out, Max took

one look at the number of cars still there, the heads he could see in the window, and kept right on going. If anyone missed him, they'd either figure he'd done exactly what he was doing, or gone to get himself good and drunk.

In any case, they'd probably be relieved to have him off doing whatever.

He'd call later tonight, or in the morning, to see what Dylan and Lily had found out.

He was hoping to have found Rachel himself before then. He knew she was partial to motels. She was kind of fastidious about cleanliness and service, but didn't like to spend exorbitant amounts of money on a room to sleep in. They'd had more than one discussion about that very thing when he'd been making reservations for their honeymoon. He'd wanted to splurge. To take her to the nicest place in Houston before they flew out to the coast for the rest of the week. She'd insisted they find a good motel near the airport.

And on that thought, sitting straight up and keeping his eye on the road, he picked up his cell phone. Ten minutes later, the trip it had taken him and Rachel more than a month to plan was completely canceled.

THE ROOM WAS CLEAN. New. Done in restfully shaded greens. Methodically, with an order that calmed her, Rachel set her suitcase on the rack left for that purpose and unpacked her toiletry case. She slipped out of her wedding gown and hung it carefully on one of the thick wooden hangers attached to the closet rod. The dress was stained along the bottom edges.

She had some stain removal wipes in her case. She'd take care of those dirt spots just as soon as she had a shower and was dressed in a pair of comfortably familiar blue jeans and one of her soft, pullover sweaters. She couldn't let the stains set for too long. It would break her heart to have ruined that beautiful dress.

Not that she needed it.

Or had a daughter to pass it on to someday.

But still, she couldn't stand to have it ruined.

Her feet stung as she slipped out of her sandals and stepped under the steaming spray. The shower had a massage head on it, and taking full advantage of the hardest setting, she tried to concentrate on her aching neck and ignore her aching feet. She'd pulled a pair of sandals out of her case as soon as she'd climbed into the truck that had brought her to San Antonio. But the trek from the church out to the FM 1022 had been rough with only a pair of ruined panty hose for protection against the stones she'd encountered.

She hadn't been going slowly enough to watch her step.

With the water pounding against the back of her neck, Rachel let her chin drop to her chest. And saw the faded red water running from around her feet, down to the drain. She'd cut her foot. Or just garnered herself a rather nasty blister or two.

In any event, she had antibiotic cream in her case. And bandage strips, too. She'd take care of her feet after she finished her shower. Before she got to the dress. She didn't want to bleed all over the new carpet in the hotel room.

She'd better check her sandals, too. They were probably stained.

And then maybe she'd see about ordering some dinner. She didn't know what was available, couldn't think of anything that sounded good, but she should eat. She hadn't had anything all day.

And sometime tonight, before she went to sleep, she had to call someone and let them know she was all right. She just couldn't figure out who to call. Ashley would demand too many answers, her father's concern would be her undoing. And Max...

God, she couldn't even think about Max. Squeezing her eyes shut against the hopeless tears that had been building all day, Rachel tried to focus again on the things she must do. Dress her feet. Clean her dress. Eat.

Anything but think about Max.

She just wasn't strong enough to do that.

A WEDDING FEAST it was not. But a drive-through burger was all the time Max could spare. His wedding night was going to be over soon. Another few hours and it would be midnight and then the dawning of a new day. And he hadn't yet found his intended. He'd set his mind to the fact that he'd find her tonight. That his wedding day wouldn't end without at least some word from Rachel.

It wasn't as if anything was bound to happen between now and morning. Rachel knew how to take care of herself. Could even be staying with a friend someplace. She had her car. Money.

Sensible, conscientious, she wasn't likely to do anything rash.

If one didn't count running away from the church on her wedding day rash.

He just couldn't figure it. All afternoon and early evening, as he'd driven the streets of San Antonio, he'd run through every moment he could remember from the past nine months. Every conversation. Every expression.

But not every touch. Those would have to wait for another day. He couldn't even think about touching Rachel tonight. He'd waited too long. Had been anticipating a much different end to this evening...

Cruising slowly through the parking lot of yet another name-brand motel, Max perused each car. Nothing. Not a single Toyota Corolla in the parking lot—let alone the midnight blue one Rachel had bought last fall when she'd come home to take the job at the Trueblood library.

Where was she?

Where in hell was she?

WHY SHE ORDERED the pizza, Rachel had no idea. She hadn't had any since her college days. And tonight of all nights was not a time she wanted to be nostalgic about anything having to do with her years in Austin. But they delivered. Maybe when it arrived and the smell permeated her room, she'd actually be able to eat.

Lying back against the propped-up pillows of her king-size bed, she flipped through the television stations, the remote hanging from her hand. After the second time through the fifteen or so stations the hotel offered, she still didn't know what was on. Didn't care.

The pizza man's arrival was a blessing. Another body to talk to, even if only for a second. A touch with reality. With a world that was carrying on as though nothing untoward had happened. As though the entire universe hadn't just fallen apart.

Rachel padded barefoot across the carpet, almost welcoming the sting of her own weight upon her bandaged feet, and grabbed the ten-dollar bill she'd laid out on the round table for two beneath her window.

Her aching feet somehow made life real. Made this moment real.

"That was quick...." Her words broke off as the blood drained from her face and her heart beat out a wild rhythm. "Max..."

He took off his cowboy hat. "May I come in?" he asked, both hands working against the brim of the hat.

"Of course." Rachel stepped back automatically. Max was here. Saving her from her private hell.

It was right. Fitting. She'd never needed anyone more in her life than she needed him.

Until she turned, closing the door of the room, and saw him standing there. His big frame took up so much of the room, she could hardly move from the door. Could hardly open her mouth to speak. His eyes, when he turned them on her, had never looked so black.

He shouldn't be there. Couldn't be there. She was running away from him.

Or, more accurately, from herself, but he was a part of that self.

"You're in a hotel."

"Yes."

"I looked at motels first."

"I wanted to be inside, with a hallway." And people she could hear—maybe even run into—in the hall. An elevator she could ride, a lobby she could go down to if the room got too claustrophobic in the middle of the night.

Another knock sounded on the door and Max swung back to the latch she'd just hooked. His dark eyes locked there.

"You expecting someone?" he asked.

There was no accusation in his words. Quiet, kind

Max wasn't like that. But she'd hurt him. It wasn't something he'd forget easily.

"Dinner," she said, when the knock sounded again. Still clutching the ten-dollar bill in her fist, she opened the door, paid the man, and brought the pizza in to the table she'd already set with a washcloth for a napkin, a small hotel glass, the ice bucket she'd filled from the machine down the hall and a couple of cans of soda.

"Let me get the other glass." Passing him again, making certain that she kept as much distance as the hotel room—and his large frame—would allow, she slipped into the bathroom and got not only another glass, but another washcloth as well.

"Have you eaten?" she asked, passing him yet a third time.

Max nodded once, his gaze following her around the room. "I had a burger. About an hour ago."

"Just a burger? That's not enough to fill you. I'm having pizza. You're welcome to a slice if you'd like."

She opened the pizza box. "I've only got a couple of sodas, but if we run out, there's a machine right down the hall..."

Embarrassed by her schoolgirl chatter, Rachel shut up, stood by the table she'd set, and stared at him. He stared right back.

"I'll have a piece," he finally said, breaking the tension that had her nerves screaming for release as he tossed his hat down on the dresser and took a seat at the table.

Rachel sat across from him, grabbed a piece of the pizza and set it on her washcloth.

"Help yourself," she said, pushing the box his way.

He took a piece, took a bite, and set the pizza down. Rachel's remained untouched.

He was going to want answers. Had to be sitting there waiting for answers. Deserved answers.

She had to try to give him some.

"I don't usually eat pizza," she said, and then realized that he knew full well what her eating habits were. Knew, too, that there was no place to order pizza in Trueblood. "Not since college."

"It's good."

She noticed that other than that one bite, he hadn't touched the piece he'd taken.

Dropping her hands to her lap, clutching them together, Rachel leaned forward. "I'm sorry, Max."

He nodded. He'd know she was sorry. He knew her. Knew how hard it was for her to hurt anyone, how hard she tried to tow the line, be what people expected her to be.

Mostly, she was fine with that. She liked how she felt about herself when she did the right thing. And she adored her father. She took pride in being the minister's daughter, in helping people, in being the one they came to when they needed a ready ear and her father wasn't available. It made her feel good to arrange meals when someone in their small town was sick or injured.

Tonight she was the sick one. Sick at heart. She needed Max so desperately. And couldn't help herself, or him, at the moment.

"I love you."

CHAPTER THREE

MAX FROWNED as Rachel told him what was in her heart. "Do you?" was all he said.

Her eyes overflowing, Rachel nodded. "More than ever, Max. Please don't doubt that."

"Doubt's a little hard to fight considering how differently this day turned out from what I'd been expecting."

Suddenly more aware than ever that she and Max were alone—in a hotel room—Rachel started to sweat. Max was a gentleman. He wasn't going to do anything inappropriate. She knew that.

She was Reverend Blair's daughter. She was eleven years Max's junior. He wasn't going to take her to bed until they were married. He'd made all that quite clear.

And Rachel had been only too eager to accept the out he'd given her all those months ago when their kisses had started leading to far more and Max had stopped himself in the middle of carrying her back to his bedroom.

Glancing from the big bed back to Max, Rachel swallowed. Hard. "This isn't about you, Max, or how I feel about you."

Hands on the table on either side of him, Max sat back in the hotel chair that his muscular body dwarfed. "Then how about you tell me what it is about."

"I..." Rachel searched her mind for anything that

she could say, anything that might help explain without delving into the things buried so deep inside of her.

''If you didn't want to get married, all you had to do was tell me.''

''I did want to!''

She didn't blame him for the look of disbelief clouding his expression.

''I do want to marry you, Max,'' she whispered, forced to look away from him. ''I just have some… issues…that I have to deal with first.'' That wasn't what she'd meant to say. Wasn't what he deserved to hear.

''These…issues. They just developed today?''

''No.''

''Last night? Yesterday?''

''No.''

His silence said far more than an entire dictionary of words could have done. That's how it was with Max, at least as far as she was concerned. He might be a quiet man, but he was always speaking to Rachel. With a look. An expression. A silence. She knew him that well.

Loved him that deeply.

''I thought I'd put it all behind me, Max. I was trying so hard to make it so, that I refused to listen to my own mind when it started sending up warnings weeks ago. I put it all down to prewedding jitters.''

''You've known for weeks that you were going to do this?''

''No!'' If nothing else, she had to make him understand. Today, tonight was as much a shock to her as it was to him. At least consciously. ''You know I'd never have let things get this far if I hadn't been completely sure that I could follow through with them.''

He was watching her, those eyes, so intelligent, so knowing, warming her even as he interrogated her. If only he'd be really angry with her instead of just harboring a bit of anger mixed in with a load of caring. This would be so much easier to bear if she could forget how badly she loved him, wanted his love.

"I can't really even tell you what happened," she said, remembering back to that morning. "I was at the church, dressed and ready, and suddenly I just snapped. I started thinking—about those…" *Tell him*, her heart said. It was the right thing to do. But just thinking around the surface of some of the things that had led her to this hotel room made it hard for her to breathe. "Issues…" she finally said. "I hadn't let myself really think about them in months, and yet there I was, thinking…"

"Are you in some kind of trouble?"

"No. It's nothing like that."

"Then what…"

Rachel leaned forward, gently laying her hands on top of his, prepared to have him brush her away. "I would have come to you if I could, Max. If there were anything you could do, I'd have come to you, you know that, don't you?"

He didn't brush her away. "I'm not sure about a hell of a lot at the moment," he said.

Max. Her rough outdoorsman. Her big, kind teddy bear. He'd spent his whole life taking care of people. This wasn't going to be easy for him. To have something wrong that he couldn't fix.

"Be sure of this," she said, squeezing his hands. "I've never loved anyone like I love you, and I'd give anything to be able to be your wife tonight. I've been looking forward to this day for more than ten years."

He didn't say anything. Just kept watching her.

Rachel pulled away. Sat back. She couldn't blame him for not jumping for joy at her declaration. In one sense, her love for him just made everything so much more difficult.

"I feel like such a jerk for doing this," she whispered. "For not realizing sooner."

"What would you have done if you had?"

She didn't know. Didn't know what she was going to do now. She'd already had counseling. She could go back for more, but she knew what they were going to tell her.

"I just need some time, Max," she said, hoping that was true.

"How much time?"

"I don't know."

Max moved suddenly, pulling her up into his arms. "This is all that matters, Rach," he said softly. "You and me, together. We can get through whatever life throws our way."

She nodded, her fingers playing nervously with the buttons on his denim shirt.

"Talk to me, babe, let me help you. Together we'll make it right, whatever it is."

She wanted to spill it all, right then and there. To have him hold her while she told him about that horrifying time in her life—and all it had left her to deal with. But when she looked up, she could hardly see him through the haze of panic. There were orange, yellow and red sparkles forming a halo around his head and shoulders.

Her heart started to pound harder. She could feel it in her temples. She wasn't going to be able to pull much more air into her lungs. Not if she couldn't back up. Find someplace inside her that was safe.

Talking wasn't safe. She had to go away from that thought. Couldn't make herself do it. It wasn't safe.

Since the night it had first happened, she'd been unable to talk about it. Later, at the hospital, they'd known, but she'd never told anyone how it happened or who was involved.

She was to blame. Nothing else mattered.

And Max was a man.

"I—I can't."

His arms fell away. Rachel shivered.

"Max..." He couldn't leave her. Not like this.

He'd sunk back down to his chair at the table. "These issues," he said. "Do you have some plan to resolve them?"

Sort of. Not really. Nothing that she wanted to acknowledge, even to herself. The nausea that had been plaguing her on and off all day returned.

Rachel shook her head.

"But you do *plan* to resolve them."

"I plan to try." Her voice cracked.

"How?"

"I don't know." It was the complete truth.

"Is there a chance they might be impossible to resolve? That you'll never be ready to marry me?"

Rachel couldn't answer that for a long time. Couldn't get a word past the lump in her throat. But he deserved to know. "Yes."

Max didn't appear surprised by her answer. He looked around the room, his frustration obvious. "How long you planning to stay here?"

"Only tonight. Probably."

"And then what? You coming back home?"

"I don't know." She couldn't even face herself at the moment, how was she going to face her father? Her dear sweet father who'd been protecting her these past couple of years. "Soon."

"You have someplace else you plan to go?"

He should be hollering at her. Telling her what a selfish, immature bitch she was. Telling her he never wanted to see her again. Telling her she didn't deserve a real man like him.

She could have handled that. Maybe.

His kindness—even mixed with the rough edge of anger—was killing her.

"I'm going to Austin." She hadn't known she'd made that decision until the words came out.

"Alone?"

"Yes."

"To see anyone in particular?"

"I don't think so."

She might take a hidden peek. But not if she had anything to say about it. She just wasn't sure how much say she had in her life at the moment. She wasn't doing anything she wanted to be doing right now.

"At least let me drive you there. You can get your car serviced as you planned."

"Max…" God, his offer was so tempting.…

"I'll leave you alone once we get there, Rach, just let me do this much for you, okay? It's been a rough day."

Max had to be doing something. That was his way of dealing with life.

She wanted to say yes. And then the walls started to close in on her again, constricting her chest, her peripheral vision. "You have to promise that you won't pressure me to answer questions I can't answer."

"Done."

"Okay."

"When were you planning to leave?"

"I don't know. In the morning, I guess." She wasn't ready. Didn't want to go. And didn't want to take Max into that sordid part of her life. Didn't want it tainting the happiness she'd found with him.

She didn't want to go there without him.

"I'll be ready." He picked up his hat.

"Where are you going to stay?"

"Here. If they've got another room."

She nodded. She should ask him to stay with her. The bed was certainly big enough. But she should have married him that morning, too. And she hadn't been able to do that, either.

"Breakfast at eight?" he asked at the door.

She nodded again.

He hesitated. "You're not going to run again, are you?"

Rachel's heart went out to him. "No, Max. I promise I won't run again. At least not without telling you."

He nodded. Rachel wished he'd yell at her. That he'd tell her how rotten she was to have done this to him. That her going had raised not only his protective instincts, but his own sense of survival as well. She wished he needed her that much.

"Max?" she called just before the door shut behind him.

He poked his head back around the edge.

"Thanks."

As she heard his steps fade down the hall, she wondered how much a woman could jerk a man around before he finally wrote her off, before she killed any love he'd ever felt for her.

And wondered how she'd survive when that happened with her and Max.

MAX CALLED DYLAN as soon as he got in a room. He wasn't on the same hall as Rachel, but he'd managed to get on the same floor, which helped him relax just a bit. He'd found her. She wasn't going anywhere. She'd promised.

"I've found her," he said as soon as Dylan picked up on his end.

"I know. She left a message with Reverend Blair, told him you were with her."

"Did she say anything else?"

"Nothing."

Damn. Picking up the base of the phone, Max paced as much as the confines of hotel room and telephone cord would allow. What in hell was going on?

"Where are you?" Dylan asked.

"A hotel in San Antonio."

"She's okay?"

"For now."

"What happened?"

Phone in hand, Max rubbed his forehead with the back of his wrist. "I don't know yet. But she's got whatever spooked her under control enough to stay put. At least for tonight."

"She didn't give you any clue what this is all about?" Dylan asked. "She walks out on your wedding and says nothing?"

Max sat on the end of the bed. "She's struggling with something pretty big, Dylan. She's no happier about any of this than I am."

"I can't believe you aren't at least a little bit pissed."

Maybe he was. Angry that she hadn't come to him with her problem, at least enough to let him know that she was having doubts about their marriage. He'd counted on the openness, the honesty between them.

"Right now all I care about is getting through this, whatever it is." The little green squares in the carpet were irritating in their sameness.

"Is she coming home with you?"

Max shook his head, and then wished he hadn't. It was beginning to hurt like hell. He needed a swig of whiskey. Could picture the bottle on the counter at home—right where he'd left it the night before.

"We're leaving for Austin in the morning."

"What's in Austin? Or who?"

If he'd felt a little better, Max would have smiled. "What's with the detective tone? We can't just take a little side trip to patch things up a bit?"

Dylan gave an embarrassed chuckle. Max could almost see the laugh lines around Dylan's eyes. The dimple that had garnered his friend his share of teasing. Neither of which had been much in evidence lately. Dylan was suffering his own bout of heartache these days.

"Sorry, man," Dylan said. "You guys have a good time."

"Yeah, well, I just didn't want you to waste any time on this when you've got more important stuff to do for Julie."

"Her birthday's on Wednesday."

"I remember."

"I'm going to Sebastian's."

"You think that's wise?" Dylan was seeing through his best friend—and husband of the woman he loved—and not finding anything at all worth befriending. Admitting that was rough on him. But even rougher was not finding the proof to keep Julie safe from her crooked husband.

"It's bound to be hard for him," Dylan said now.

"You really think so?"

Max couldn't even pretend a civil sympathy for the man Dylan was investigating. He'd never liked Sebastian Cooper. The man had double-crossed Dylan long before now, in Max's opinion. He'd done Dylan wrong when he'd married the woman Dylan loved.

"You know, Max, sometimes I wonder why I didn't just decide to stay right here at the ranch like you. I like the life you've made for yourself. You know exactly where you're going. You're in control."

"And that was completely evident this morning."

"Yeah, well…"

"You'd never have been happy ranching, Dylan. And you did come back to the ranch—both you and Lily. You were a great cop. And you're an even better detective. There's no measuring the joy you and Lily bring people, reuniting families that might otherwise have been lost to each other forever."

"I'm just glad you and Rachel didn't end up being another of our statistics," Dylan returned. "Enjoy your trip."

Reminding his friend to be careful on Wednesday at Sebastian's, Max rang off. Enjoyment wasn't even a consideration of tomorrow's trip. He was dreading it.

He had absolutely no idea what he was going to find in Austin. Or what he could do about whatever it was. He was completely unprepared—something Max made it a point never to be.

Rachel had said many things that evening, but the one that he just kept hearing, over and over, was that there was a possibility that whatever was bothering her might never be resolved. She might never marry him.

He went to sleep with that thought. And was up on and off for most of the night.

SHE DIDN'T KNOW what she hoped to find in Austin. Or why she wasn't just driving herself there in her own car. This journey was a personal one.

Glancing at Max as he drove, his cowboy hat almost scraping the top of the truck, she wasn't sure what to do with him. What to say to him. She knew only what she couldn't say. She'd tried a couple of times that morning. Had thought she'd gotten herself to a place where she could talk to Max about the past and not pass out before the telling was done. But each time she'd drawn a breath, intending to begin, the panic had set in. She had to go this one alone.

She was a strong woman. She'd get through this. Somehow.

She didn't know where to tell him to turn off when they reached the town where her life had changed so drastically.

There really wasn't anyplace she could think of to go. The problem was inside herself.

And for some reason she had to be in Austin.

"You hungry?" Max asked, glancing her way.

Rachel shook her head. She'd barely eaten any of the breakfast he'd insisted she order. She certainly didn't want to have to choke down anything else just three hours later. "But if you want lunch, go ahead. I'll have a soda or something."

What she wanted was a beer. At eleven-thirty in the morning.

But Rachel Blair—the minister's daughter—didn't

drink anything stronger than the solar tea she made on hot summer days.

"I can wait."

Rachel nodded, growing more and more uncomfortable. Max wasn't his normal self, either. A big man with a big appetite, he never waited to eat.

And he always played the stereo when he drove—country tunes. There'd been no music that morning.

He was wearing his uniform of jeans and button-down shirt, though it was dark green that morning rather than the denim one he'd had on the night before. She'd always loved how comfortable he was in his clothes, in his tall, muscular body.

Silence stretched out between them again—as it had most of the morning. Other than the passing scenery, which they'd both seen many times before, there was nothing to talk about. Their old life was a sensitive subject at the moment since neither of them knew what parts of it even existed anymore. And who knew where they were headed?

Rachel watched the green swipes of color whiz past her window. She felt herself growing edgier the closer they got to Austin. She should be alone. She should really be alone. Why wasn't she strong enough to send him away?

"We're almost there." Rachel jumped when Max broke the silence several moments later. Rubbing her hands along denim-clad thighs, she scrunched her toes inside her tennis shoes and nodded. She knew one reason she wasn't sending him home. Because Max needed this. His life had just fallen apart and he needed to feel like he was doing something.

She couldn't deny him that.

"What turnoff you want me to take?"

Seeing a scattering of dim stars in her peripheral vision, Rachel counted how many blue cars were on the road with them and named an exit she'd never taken before.

But it was one that she could picture quite clearly in her mind's eye. One she could feel in her heart.

An exit she'd never planned to take as long as she lived. What in the hell was the matter with her?

She needed to take herself off someplace far away where there were no memories. To heal.

"Are we going to the university?" Max asked. He'd promised not to ask questions she couldn't answer, and he'd been true to his word.

"Maybe." She hadn't thought about it. Didn't see much point in reliving those memories. "Later."

She didn't know how to put those memories to rest.

She could hardly speak. Could hardly breathe. Her stomach was fluttering. She felt sick.

Max turned off the freeway. "Where to?"

She didn't know. "Right, I guess."

Light-headed, Rachel could hardly bear to look out the window. Didn't want to see the city, the sunshine.

What am I doing?

She knew the address by heart. She'd never been on the street. Never seen the house. But she knew the address.

"Turn here," she told Max as they approached the residential street she hadn't really even decided to look for.

"We stopping to see someone?"

"No!" She was shaking so hard she was afraid he'd notice.

He sent her a curious glance, but said nothing.

Judging by the numbers on the curb, it would be

around that bend. Just around that bend. Part of her life was there.

Would anyone be outside? Would she finally see...

Rachel's heart thudded in her chest when she saw the For Sale sign, the flyers piled up on the doorstep an obvious indication of vacancy.

It couldn't be for sale.

Trying not to show any interest in one house over another, she didn't look back as they passed.

"Turn here," she said, almost woodenly, let down beyond imagination.

Max turned. She felt his glance on her, but didn't turn her head from the window. She couldn't.

He drove silently, turning when she instructed. True to his word, he didn't ask questions. But he knew.

Knew that something had upset her terribly.

And she couldn't tell him what. She hadn't even told her father that part of the nightmare. He'd suffered for her so much already.

Besides, it was the last part that had robbed her, the minister's daughter, of her faith. A faith she'd never regained. And if her father had known, he'd probably have lost his as well. She hadn't been able to do that to him. Paying the price herself had seemed the most loving choice.

Now she wondered.

Had she instead robbed him of the chance to give counsel? Counsel she might desperately have needed?

Had she made a mistake, leaving a part of herself in Austin? Was that why she hadn't been able to marry Max?

Or was this all just backlash from the act of violence that had stolen her innocence?

She didn't even realize the truck had stopped until

she felt Max slide across the seat. He pulled her into his arms without a word, and without a word, she went. Whether it was right or wrong, fair or not, she needed him in ways he couldn't possibly understand.

"I'm here if you need to talk," he said.

She didn't. Couldn't. The words simply closed her throat.

"I promised I wouldn't ask, and I won't," he continued a moment later, his voice soft. "But I'm with you on this, babe. Whatever it is, I'm with you."

The most Rachel could do was clutch his shirt, but she did so with both hands. He was with her then, but would he still be when he found out all that she hadn't told him? Would she ever find a way to tell him? Would she ever be that healthy, that whole again?

She wasn't the person he thought her to be.

And if he did stand by her—which, knowing Max, he probably would, if for no other reason than to help her—could she ever be a real wife to him? He'd made it clear that though he'd waited to make love to her, the waiting had been extremely difficult. At this point, sex was the only thing she was certain he needed from her.

And sex was the one thing she wasn't certain she could give him.

CHAPTER FOUR

SEBASTIAN COOPER never stopped working anymore. The fact that it was Sunday night made no difference to him. The end of the tunnel was approaching fast and he had to find Julie before it all fell apart. Before Dylan found her.

"You get anything on that Devereaux woman?" he barked into the phone. He was in his office, but didn't even notice the plush surroundings. His attention was turned inward. Focused on his goals. Always focused.

The gruff voice on the other end of the phone gave him some bunk about swamps.

"I don't care, you get that?" he said more softly, leaving spittle on his lip. "Find her."

"Yes, boss."

"You get her by the end of the week or you're through."

Really through. At this point in the game Sebastian didn't just fire people. And he didn't make idle threats.

"We'll find her."

Satisfied, Sebastian hung up. He had the best men in the business working for him. They'd get the Devereaux woman, and through her, they'd get Julie. Sebastian had a feeling about that woman. And his feelings had never led him wrong before. Everything was going to work out just fine. Better than planned. And it would be easy street from there. For the rest of his life Sebastian would only have to give orders and eat up the little guys. Finally life would be exactly as it should be.

So what if Dylan was good at what he did? He might be a star investigator, but he'd never been as good as Sebastian. At anything. Why start worrying about his best friend now?

Sebastian had everything—including Julie—under complete control.

MAX WAS UP with the sun on Monday morning. He'd spent the day before driving Rachel all around Austin. She'd been quiet, but had shown him the dorm she'd lived in for the four years she'd been gone, pointed out buildings where she'd taken classes, places she'd eaten regularly. After a quick supper, which Rachel barely touched, he'd left her at the door of the motel room he'd obtained for her. The room adjoining his.

He'd spent a restless, frustrating night caged inside a room that was far too small. He'd been tempted to go out—to take a good long walk if nothing else, or find a bar to plant his butt in for a while. But he'd been loath to leave in case Rachel needed anything.

He was her only transportation.

And, he hoped, her friend.

Friend. A far cry from the lover he'd expected to be when he'd arranged to have this week off work.

Knocking on her door at six-forty-five, only fifteen minutes before the time they'd set to meet for breakfast, he shifted his weight from one cowboy boot to the other. Hopefully this day, whatever it held, would bring some answers.

The latch finally clicked and he heard the chain slide away from the door.

"Hi." She looked worn, as though she hadn't slept well, but beautiful just the same.

"Did you sleep at all?" he asked, leaning on the doorjamb while she collected her stuff. His was already stowed in the back of the truck.

She wasn't meeting his eyes. "Some."

Max took the bag from her and set it up beside his. Unlocking her door, he left it open and went around to his side of the truck.

"Breakfast?" he asked as he slid in beside her.

She nodded, fastening her seat belt.

"You going to eat something this time?" She'd hardly eaten the day before. Probably even less the day before that.

He was doing a damn fine job of taking care of her.

Looking up at him, she tried to grin and he caught just a glimpse of the imp who'd followed him around for years. "Yes, I'll eat. I'd hate to have you think you're falling down on your job."

She knew him well. Satisfied, Max set about finding them a diner that was open and looked better than greasy. He wasn't averse to a little grease, but Rachel was a lot more health conscious than he was.

It felt great to have a destination in mind. To be in charge of their destiny. Even if only for the next half hour or so.

"What's on the agenda for today?" he asked, once Rachel had finished almost an entire bowl of oatmeal and was still working on the English muffin that had come with it in the fifties-style diner he'd found.

He wasn't supposed to ask questions. And he wouldn't. He wanted Rachel to come to him on her own with whatever was troubling her. But a guy had to have some kind of a plan with all those hours stretching out before him.

"I need to find Mr. and Mrs. James Emerson."

Max set his fork, the last bite of egg stuck on the end, down on his plate. They were getting somewhere.

"Okay," he said gently. She was like an injured bird, sitting there. One wrong move and she might fly away and leave him. Or fall off her perch permanently. He'd never seen her so inside out fragile.

God, what had happened to her?

And how could he not have seen these demons that were haunting her before now?

She nibbled on her muffin, looked up at him, and then away.

She had something to tell him.

He wasn't sure he wanted to hear what it was.

"Did we go by their house yesterday?" he finally prompted.

She nodded. "It was deserted. For sale."

He'd felt her stiffen beside him when they'd approached that house, seen the lost look in her eyes. She'd shut down as soon as they'd turned off that street.

"Do you know where to look for them?"

She shook her head, her long hair silky and fragile looking as it swept her shoulders. He'd been dreaming for months of that hair cascading down over his naked body.

"I was hoping we could find a library." she said. "Look on the Internet for a listing."

"If their move was recent, they might not be there."

"I know."

"Is there any other way we can contact them? Anyone you know who might know where they are?"

Dropping the muffin in her nearly empty cereal bowl, Rachel licked her lips. "Maybe."

Nothing more.

"Probably."

Clamping down on his jaw so that the questions ready to spew forth would stay put, Max paid the bill, tipped the waitress, waited while Rachel asked for directions to the nearest library, then followed her back out to the truck.

This wasn't about him. It was about Rachel. About being there for her. He loved her, but he could take care of himself.

It promised to be another long day.

MAX PULLED INTO a shopping center parking lot and called Dylan to have his friend run a quick check on the Emersons. After a morning of dead ends, Rachel was feeling a little less threatened by what might be just around the corner. She and Max sat in the truck and chatted while they waited for Dylan's call back. Though Max was a naturally quiet man, his intelligence was sharp, his conversation stimulating. He always came up with insights that surprised Rachel. And bits of obscure knowledge that left her wondering where he'd found them.

For now, until she had more information to go on here in Austin, she was at the end of the road. It felt great not to have something pulling her to places she didn't want to go. Glorious to know that there was nowhere she *could* go even if she wanted to.

All these years she'd had the sense that her past was out there just waiting for her to get up the courage. To quit being so weak. And now that she was here, it wasn't waiting.

Maybe it never had been.

"Max?" she asked, wishing this were sometime last week so she'd have been able to reach over and run her hand along his jean-clad leg.

"Yeah?" His black eyes were shaded as he looked over at her.

"I just want you to know how much this means to me, your hanging around like this. I know this isn't right, isn't fair, expecting you to just follow me blindly around...."

He reached over and put one callused finger against her lips. "Rach, it's obvious that you aren't ready—or even able—to talk. You practically passed out on me last night when I asked you for answers. I may make my living raising animals, but I know a bit about human beings, too. There are times when the psyche just doesn't cooperate, no matter how much we want it to."

"I want it to," she whispered, amazed all over again at how much Max saw, how much he understood.

"And that's enough for now. We're engaged to be married," he said. "Right and fair doesn't come into it. Who else should be here helping you?"

"So...you still think we're engaged?"

He glanced at the diamond he'd placed on her finger a few short months before. "Don't you?"

"I guess." She didn't know what to think. She'd thought about taking the ring off, but with him there with her, it hadn't seemed right. "I want to be." But how did you promise to marry a man you weren't sure you could marry?

He was tapping one hand against the steering wheel, watching a woman load shopping bags into her car.

Chest tight, she asked, "Do you?"

He looked over at her. "I want to marry you, Rachel."

His tone put a but on the end of that sentence, which was compounded by the fact that other than to offer comfort now and then, he wasn't touching her at all. They hadn't kissed since the night before the wedding...

"Go on," she prompted.

And jumped when his cell phone rang.

"Yeah," he said into the little black mouthpiece.

Holding her breath, Rachel waited. Had Dylan found the Emersons already? Where were they? How far away from where Rachel sat right now?

"When?"

Stomach tight, she watched Max's frown grow deeper.

How much could Dylan have found out during that short period of time? She'd worked with him. Helped him regularly with his research at the library. He was impressively good at ferreting out information from the most unlikely sources, but it had only been about twenty minutes.

"Uh-huh."

Opening the glove box, Max grabbed a little black notebook and a pen. He scribbled something down.

"Go on."

She was going to be sick. She wished she hadn't eaten the sandwich he'd talked her into for lunch.

Was this it then? She was really going to know where they were? And what if they were close? Was she going to see them?

Was she ready?

Would she ever be ready?

Oh, God. She couldn't do this.

She couldn't see what Max had written. Did he have a phone number?

She couldn't call them with him sitting right there.

"Yeah, man. Thanks."

Her time was up.

Max's movements were very deliberate. He pushed the button to end the call. Set the phone carefully in the cubby in the dash. Tore the piece of paper out of the notebook and returned both the book and the pen to the glove box, closing it gently. Frozen, she sat watching him.

What did he know?

He started the truck, but didn't put it into gear. Then he looked at Rachel.

"How well did you know the Emersons?"

"N-n…" Rachel swallowed, concentrated on something simple, unthreatening, just as she'd been taught. There were eight eyelets on Max's boots. She tried again. "Not well."

He seemed relieved by that. "You weren't particularly close to them?"

She shook her head. Of course, that depended on how you defined close. She had only met them a couple of times. But what they'd shared…

"Did Dylan find out where they are?" She wanted to put her hands over her ears. She didn't want to know.

She had to know.

"They were killed, babe, in a car accident on the 35. It happened on New Year's Day. A drunk driver. It was instant."

Dead. They were dead.

Her peripheral vision grew dark. A part of her knew

this was worse then the stars. It was all closing in on her.

That nice couple. They'd only been thirty years old. Nancy had just passed the bar exam. James was a doctor. A pediatrician...

Had just the two of them died? Or was someone else in the car? Were they all dead?

Ohmigod. She couldn't be dead. Suddenly, Rachel found herself praying. *Please, dearest God in Heaven, don't let her be dead.*

Vaguely aware of Max, she felt him beside her, against her. He took one of her hands in both of his.

"H-how m-many?" she choked out, barely seeing the LED clock readout right in front of her.

"How many what, babe?" His voice was softer than normal, coming from far, far away.

"In the car. How many were there?" If only the darkness would just come. Take her away.

"It was just the two of them. The other driver wasn't hurt."

The relief was so strong tears sprang to her eyes. Her entire body felt like it was floating—held down on the seat only by the sorrow she still felt. The Emersons had saved her at a time when she'd thought herself beyond saving. They'd found a way to reach her in her hell, to make her feel good about something.

They'd had their whole lives ahead of them.

She isn't dead. Ruby hadn't been in the car with them.

Her mind raced, from one possibility to the next, settling nowhere. Aware of nothing.

"There's more." Max's voice surprised her. She'd felt so alone.

"What?" she asked, looking over. Sometime in the

past few moments he'd slid next to her. Was still holding her hand. Gently rubbing the back of it with a callused thumb. She'd seen him rub the belly of a mare in labor with as much gentleness. She'd been fourteen at the time.

That's when she'd fallen in love with Max Santana.

"They had a baby, Rach."

The blood drained from her face. How had Dylan found that out so quickly?

"Her name is Ruby. She's been put in foster care."

She was in foster care. Her dear, sweet, unplanned and unwanted baby was in foster care.

Her baby.

Not the Emersons any longer.

She looked up at Max, studied his face, his expression. His eyes were filled with compassion, with questions, but not with shock. Max didn't know.

"Do you know where she is?" she asked, the words sticking in her throat.

"I have the address and phone number of the caseworker. That's the best Dylan could do on such short notice."

Rachel nodded and held out her free hand. "May I have it?"

Silently he put the folded notepaper in her palm.

One look at the name, and Rachel didn't need to read the address. She knew it by heart, too. It was a place she'd been too many times over those nightmarish months, interviewing, searching for just the right parents.

"Would you like me to take you there?" Max asked. "I'm sure they'll be able to tell you more about what happened. If you need to know more."

She didn't even think about it. Couldn't think.

Couldn't trust herself to handle the thoughts. "Yes. Please."

Without another word, Max slid back beneath the steering wheel, put the truck in drive and headed out into the busy Monday afternoon traffic. It was only three o'clock, Rachel thought. Stella would still be at work.

Rachel had spent more evenings than she could count sitting there with her. Sometimes looking through reports of potential families, sometimes just trying to escape her demons. Stella hadn't just been her caseworker. She'd been a good friend to a frightened young woman who'd gone from innocence to hell in the space of a fifteen-minute act of violence.

CHAPTER FIVE

THE ADDRESS Dylan had given him was on the other side of Austin, close to the university. The streets were familiar as he and Rachel had combed them earlier that morning, looking for he knew not what.

Nor did he know if they'd found what they'd been after.

The questions were racking up quicker than his debts on an off night of poker. But he didn't need answers until she was ready to give them. He was there to help her. This wasn't about him.

But who in hell were the Emersons? Their death had hit her hard. Yet he wasn't sure how to console her. Was it just the tragedy of lives taken too young, or was her grief more personal?

And if it was personal, why in hell hadn't he ever heard of them?

Had Rachel been involved with James Emerson? In love with him maybe? Had he been married then? If he had, Rachel couldn't have known. She'd never have knowingly had an affair with a married man.

Maybe that was it. It would have killed her to find out that was exactly what she had been doing.

He glanced toward his silent companion, wishing he could be wherever she was, telling himself not to feel hurt by her desertion. He needed to understand, not dwell on feeling shut out.

He was used to the feeling, though. He'd been on the outside looking in his entire life. He liked it that way. It put him in control.

Rachel turned her head away. Sniffed. Damn. She was crying.

Had she known about the child, too, before today? Had the baby come along while Rachel and James were still involved? Had he told her his wife was pregnant and ended the affair?

Things were starting to make some sort of sense. If Rachel had indeed found herself involved in something so sordid, it could have shaken her this badly—left her unable to handle life.

The counseling building was nondescript—one-story brick on the edge of campus. It looked just like a hundred other such buildings in a hundred other towns.

Max looked eagerly toward the front door as he parallel parked. In that door were some answers. Finally.

Surely, without asking, he'd be able to derive from the conversation just what Rachel's relationship to the Emersons really was. He'd find out how accurate he'd been.

Then he'd set about convincing Rachel that none of that mattered. It didn't change how he felt about her— other than maybe a tiny bit of disappointment that he wasn't going to be her first and only lover.

Once he convinced her it didn't matter, he'd convince her that just because one man was a scum, it didn't make him one. If Emerson had actually taken her innocence without letting her know he was married, it could have affected Rachel this strongly. Some women might have taken it in their stride, but not Rachel, a Christian girl raised by a minister father in a small town where the worst thing that happened was the occasional drunk making a scene.

Emerson's action could explain Rachel's cold feet on their wedding day. She might have been afraid to commit herself to a lifetime with Max. To trust another man with her heart. If she'd only come to him, he could have shown her she didn't need to be afraid. He wasn't going to let her down. He'd always been honest with her, and he would be until the day he died.

Of course, coming to him with something like this would probably have been harder for her than marrying him. It was obvious she needed to talk to him. And just as obvious that something inside, something stronger than her will, was stopping her.

She didn't make any move to get out when he stopped the truck. Just sat there looking lost. Frightened. She took a deep breath as though searching inside herself for the strength to get through the next moments.

"You ready?" he prompted when it looked like she was going to sit there fighting with herself for the rest of the afternoon.

She nodded and reached for the door handle, then stopped and looked at him.

"I need to do this alone, Max."

His heart dropped. "You're sure?" he asked. He was there to help her, and if this was what she needed, he would give it to her.

She ran her tongue along her bottom lip and looked toward the glass door with the name of the Family Services center emblazoned in big gold letters.

"I'm sure," she said.

"I'll wait here."

Nodding, Rachel opened her door, looking back at

him as she slid out. "You're sure you're okay?" she asked. At that moment, her eyes were filled with compassion. For him.

He wasn't the one who needed it.

"Of course I'm sure. Go."

She went.

Max leaned back in the seat, laying his head on the rest, closing his eyes. He was damn glad, as always, that his role in life was being the caretaker. He might spend a lot of time on the outside looking in, but at least this way he always knew what was expected of him.

With one last peek, he saw Rachel pull open that glass door and disappear inside. She'd probably be there for a few minutes. Crossing his arms against his chest, he attempted to discipline himself to sleep. But instead, he spent the next half hour fighting with himself and the very odd desire to be on the inside looking out for once.

This wasn't about him.

It was about Rachel.

He needed to be very clear on that.

"RACHEL! How *are* you?"

At least one thing about Stella Ramirez hadn't changed a bit in the past year. She jumped up to give Rachel a hug hello.

Rachel embarrassed herself by holding on too tight—for too long.

"You look great!" Stella said, eventually pulling back to give Rachel a once-over. "Your hair's still as long and beautiful as always, and you've lost those shadows under your cheekbones. Going home to Trueblood was obviously the right decision."

Nodding, Rachel managed a tremulous smile and took her old familiar seat on the couch in Stella's office. Stella sat sideways on the couch, one knee pulled up, as she faced Rachel.

"So tell me what's been going on in your life. What changes has the year brought?"

Stella's chocolate eyes peered at her, full of curiosity—and caring. The caseworker was wearing her black hair up in a bun and had on the same type of plain slacks and blouse she'd always worn. She was still slightly husky without being plump—in fact, she hadn't really changed at all. Yet she looked so different to Rachel. So far away.

She filled the other woman in on her new life—the job that she loved. For the moment, she left out the part about being engaged to be married, about running out on her own wedding.

She also didn't mention the man waiting outside for her.

"So what brings you to Austin?" Stella asked when Rachel grew silent. The other woman had sobered considerably with that last question, almost as though she suspected that Rachel knew about Ruby.

"You know, after the first couple of letters, I chose not to receive any more," Rachel said slowly.

Stella nodded. "They're supposed to be a comfort, but many times they're more painful than no word at all."

Head bowed, Rachel stared at the diamond on her finger. Caught up in the moment, she'd forgotten it was there. But Stella, sharp as she was, couldn't have missed the glittering stone. So why hadn't she asked about it?

Calming herself with steady breaths, with visions of

lush green ranch lands and cool breezes, Rachel searched for the right words.

"I ran out on my wedding." Not what she'd wanted to say at all.

If she felt any surprise, Stella covered it well. "Recently?"

"Two days ago."

"Does anyone know where you are?"

"Yes."

"You want to talk about it?"

"You don't seem surprised."

"I'm not, not really," Stella paused, and her eyes when they met Rachel's were serious. "You've got some pretty heavy-duty baggage. It takes a while to rid yourself of the effects."

Panic sliced through Rachel. "I went through all of the counseling. They said I was ready to get on with my life."

"You are," Stella said softly, adamantly. "But getting on with your life means just this, taking that next step *and* finding a way to make it gel with your past. Getting married is a huge threat to anyone's equilibrium. But with you, it also forces you to face some very natural fears and aversions, brings out things that otherwise might remain stagnant."

"Like the fear of making love with the man I love?"

"That, yes."

"But I felt real, honest-to-goodness desire for him," Rachel cried. She'd thought she had the past beat. That she was as normal as any woman embarking on the rest of her life.

"That's good!" Stella said, her face breaking into a wide grin. "Some women who've been victims of violence never get turned on again. They're never able to relax enough to have an orgasm.''

Rachel might have been embarrassed if she and Stella hadn't already been through far more intimate honesties. Stella had been with Rachel through the worst night and morning of her life. And those moments afterward when the feeling of loss, of being cut adrift and entirely alone, had almost consumed her to the point of death.

She frowned. ''But since I'm obviously not one of them, what happened?''

Leaning forward, Stella took one of Rachel's hands in her own. ''A part of you is ready, Rach, healed and moving on. And another part of you still needs time. It's that simple. And that complex.''

''I'm caught in a state of flux.''

''In a sense.''

''Might it be permanent?''

''It might be.'' Stella stopped, grabbed a couple of bottles of water from the small refrigerator behind her desk, and came back to the couch, handing one to Rachel. ''Part of your psyche still remembers what happened too vividly. It's reacting instinctively, which made you act instinctively as well.''

''By bolting.''

''Yes.''

''And having a resurgence of the panic attacks every time I try to talk about it?''

''Yes.''

''So how do I help me not remember so vividly? Is time supposed to take care of that, too?''

She'd learned a lot about time as the greatest of all healers in her sessions on coping and grieving.

''It might.'' Stella held her water bottle between

both hands, twisting it back and forth. "And it might not."

Not daring to sip from her own drink in case the liquid wouldn't slide past the blockage in her throat, Rachel pulled at the paper on the bottle instead. "Is there anything I can do?" she asked, meeting Stella's eyes. The other woman had to know that she was determined to get through this.

"I'm assuming from what you've just said that you haven't told your fiancé about your past."

Stella barely paused long enough for Rachel's quietly uttered "No."

That didn't seem to surprise the caseworker. "He knows nothing?"

She shook her head.

"Not even about Ruby?"

She shook her head again.

"And right there's your first step, my dear. How can you possibly trust a man to temper himself to your needs when he doesn't even know you have any?"

"I'd rather he not do anything special," Rachel said. She'd thought long and hard about that. "I just want the past behind me. To be normal. I don't want him thinking about...you know...when he's making love to me."

"Don't you think he has a right to know?"

"Of course I do." She paused, quite certain the caseworker already knew what she was about to say. "But each time I try to tell him, I lose it."

"Would it help if I told you that was perfectly normal, too?"

"I don't know. Maybe. Probably not. We don't talk about his former relationships."

"What happened to you could hardly be considered

a relationship. You want to bring him here? Maybe being here will make it easier for you.''

Rachel started to shiver. And to sweat. ''I can't.'' She cringed, inside and out. Just thinking about telling Max, about having him know made her close up inside. She felt cramped beyond bearing, claustrophobic. As though, if she took Max back with her to that awful night, everything good and beautiful in life would be gone forever.

''It's been my experience that if you're ever going to heal completely, it will have to come out eventually.''

''You think I'm still running—not dealing with the past.'' Then what in hell had all the honesty, all the remembering, all the facing things been about?

Stella shook her head. ''You've approached the entire incident in a primarily healthy way,'' she said. ''You've faced your internal demons—the ones that are yours alone, that only you can face—and you've gone on with your life, involving yourself in meaningful associations, not shying away from emotional closeness...''

Rachel started to breathe more easily as Stella's words rolled over her. She was okay. She was going to be okay.

''But eventually, Rach, you're going to have to learn to talk about what happened to you. Because only when you can deal with it in terms of the other people in your life will you ever truly set yourself free.''

''And you think that will take care of my little aversion to my wedding day?''

''Maybe.'' Stella took a long drink from the bottle she held. ''More likely, it will be your fiancé's reaction to the news, his willingness to coax your sexual responses out of hiding that will do the trick. If he's a good man…''

''He's the absolute best.''

Stella smiled. ''…If he's smart.''

''A lot smarter than I am.''

''That's saying a lot.''

Rachel tended to the little pile of label paper she'd amassed on her lap.

''If he is truly these things, then he'll be patient with you, Rach. He'll stop the minute you need to stop. Make you feel safe *before* he tries to take you anyplace else. He'll give you the measure of security that will allow you to let him love you the way you were meant to be loved.''

Rachel looked up again, tears brimming in her eyes. ''You really think there's hope for me?''

''I do,'' Stella said. ''No guarantees, of course—'' she shrugged ''—but hope, certainly.''

''Thanks,'' Rachel sighed. ''You have no idea how badly I needed to hear that.''

''But first you have to tell him.''

Oh, yeah. That.

''So how do I make myself tell him? How do I keep my body from closing up every time I try?''

''You just keep trying. And if all else fails, bring him here to me.''

''I'll think about it,'' Rachel said. And she would. Knowing herself, she'd think of little else. But that still didn't mean she'd be able to do as Stella was instructing. Something was going to have to change inside her before she could have that conversation with Max.

Something that would keep her from choking on her words before she ever got one out.

''Remember, Rachel, you're doing this for both of

you. Until he knows about your past, he doesn't know all of you. Instead of being able to understand and share a certain reaction you may have to the content of a movie, to a particular story in a newspaper, to dark rooms or a particular type and color of blanket, to that certain scent of aftershave, to a baby's cry, he'll be oblivious, carrying on as though all were normal, when you're screaming inside. Or fighting the urge to run. Or throw up.''

Rachel gave a watery, exhausted grin. "I don't throw up anymore.''

"Not recently, anyway,'' Stella said knowingly. "But if something affected you strongly enough…''

"Okay.'' Rachel held up her hand, thinking of her wedding day when she'd been playing tag with the nausea. "I get your point. And it's a good one. I'll keep trying.''

But she knew she still couldn't do it. Stella's pressure, however well-intentioned, had the walls closing in again, until there was nothing but that awful dread. Until death started to feel better than living.

She couldn't go back there again.

"There's something else I have to do,'' she blurted, more harshly than she'd intended.

The defensiveness, the survival instincts she was usually able to control were controlling her.

"What's that?'' Stella asked gently.

"Ruby.''

Stella sat back, leaning into the corner of the couch. She set her empty water bottle on the floor at her feet. "I wondered if that was why you were here.''

"Is she really in foster care?'' The words flew out in a rush. There was no way to go at this gently. To take it slow or easy. There was nothing easy about it.

Stella's brown eyes were shadowed with concern. "She's in a temporary home at the moment, waiting for a more permanent placement."

"Is she being adopted again?" The words stuck in her throat.

Her earrings jangled as Stella shook her head. "Not yet. She's not a baby anymore. The older the kids get, the longer it takes to find them a family."

"But she's not even two yet!"

"I know." Stella's tone was filled with tenderness. "We'll find her a family, I'm certain of that. But without the long waiting list of preapproved families, the process takes a bit longer. We'll want to match her with parents that share her features, if we can. Red hair. Green eyes."

Red hair. Green eyes.

Concentrate on the facts. Not the emotions. There was information she needed. No feelings allowed.

Breathe. In through the nose; out through the mouth. Just like she'd learned. Study the threads in the carpet, find a pattern, count color sequences.

"This more permanent placement you're waiting for, it's only a stopping point until you find a family to adopt her?"

"That's right." Stella's nod was short, succinct, as though she wanted to spend as little time on the subject as possible.

"Why can't she stay where she is until an adoptive family is found?" The little girl had been snatched from her home, from everything and everyone familiar to her, put in a home with one family, only to be moved to another family—and waiting to be moved to a fourth family....

Rachel was crying so fiercely inside, she couldn't

believe her eyes were dry. She wondered if perhaps she'd cried all the tears she had to cry. Maybe the suffering was deeper now. Beyond tears.

"The accident was almost five months ago," Stella reminded her. "She was put in a permanent foster home at that time, but the couple is now going through a messy divorce and could no longer keep her. We had to put her somewhere on little notice and the only opening we had was with a woman who only keeps babies and toddlers for short durations. She's too afraid of becoming attached."

Make that five homes by the time Ruby was done moving. And the little girl, really a baby still, was with a woman who didn't want to become attached.

"The Emersons didn't have any family?"

Why hadn't she known that? Made a large extended family a requirement?

"James's mother is still alive, but they've been estranged for years. He'd refused to disown his father during his parents' divorce and I guess she never forgave him. She wasn't at the funeral. And there was a brother—on Nancy's side—who's single, in the air force and stationed overseas. He's never even met Ruby. Had no means of caring for her."

Rachel nodded silently.

"The Emersons had gone out for New Year's Eve. A neighbor girl was baby-sitting Ruby, and her family kept her for the first twenty-four hours after the accident, until it could be established that there was no place for her to go. No one who was going to step forward to care for her. The state had no other choice but to take her into custody."

The pain, when it returned, slashed with renewed vengeance.

Rachel's jeans, almost a size too big, were cutting off her breath, the collar of her shirt half choking her.

"Can I see her?"

That's what she'd been going to do the day before. Somehow, in the back of her mind, she thought that she'd be okay if only she could catch a glimpse of the little girl. To say the goodbyes she'd been unable to say before.

"I don't think that's wise." Stella's voice was firm.

"Is it illegal?"

"Because you retained the right to contact, not really, but it's highly unusual. There are no procedures for allowing that contact when there are no parents."

"But that doesn't mean I can't see her."

Stella leaned forward again, her eyes deadly serious. "Rachel, please, don't do this to yourself. There's nothing to be gained."

A little girl, not even two years old, was being shuffled around like a sack of dirty laundry. Five homes. In less than two years, she'd have bonded with five different families.

Unless her young survival instincts kicked in and she quit bonding altogether.

Rachel turned cold. And then hot. She started to shake. The world was dark everywhere except for the pinpoint where Stella's face remained.

"I don't just want to see her," she whispered. "I want to take her. Home. To live with me."

CHAPTER SIX

STELLA DIDN'T GASP. Didn't rear back in shock. That reaction was reserved for the being who existed in that place deep inside Rachel—the person who hid out, frightened and alone, who had just heard her own words.

"I can't let you do that, Rachel."

"You don't—"

With a hand on her leg, Stella forestalled her. "Not without talking with someone first."

"Agreed. I'd want to do that anyway. I know there'll be adjustments and I want to be prepared."

Who was that woman speaking so calmly? Rachel was panicked, scared to death. What was she doing?

"Please stop and think about what you're saying, Rach," Stella said, sounding more like a friend than a social worker. "You made your decision—the right one, I believe—over two years ago. You've gone on, made a good life for yourself, put the past behind you...."

"Have I?" Rachel interrupted, a bitterness she rarely felt lacing her words. "I can't marry the man I love more than life itself, and you consider that 'going on'?"

"Give it time...."

"Is there a law against me taking her?"

"No."

"You're her caseworker. You've certainly got enough on me to satisfy any investigation."

"We'd need to do some recent fact-finding, look at your job, your home, your family, everything about your current situation."

"I'm living at home with my father, the minister." Rachel said, her voice dry, mechanical. Her father, who knew nothing about the child. He'd suffered so much already. One night, when he'd thought Rachel was asleep, she'd heard him railing against the Heavenly Father he served so faithfully. His anger had frightened Rachel almost more than the tragedy she'd lived through. And when, after all she'd been through, she ended up pregnant anyway, causing her to lose every ounce of the faith that had seen her through that far, she'd remembered her father's earlier anger with God and hadn't been able to tell him about the baby. She couldn't risk the news affecting him like it had affected her. She couldn't rob him of his faith.

Her father was a minister. And what kind of ministering could he do to the hundreds of people who relied on him if he lost his faith?

Rachel suddenly became aware of her surroundings. The companion who was sitting there waiting for her. Only then did Rachel realize she'd stopped speaking in midsentence. "I live with my father," she said again, "not with my fiancé. It's a four-bedroom house next door to the church. I work five days a week, eight hours a day, but am due vacation and will take as much time as I need besides. I was going to quit eventually, anyway, after I got married and started a family...."

She broke off. A family. Starting a family. She and Max had talked about it—briefly—in general terms. It had been the best she could do. Another thing she'd shied away from. There'd been so many. She was only now beginning to realize...

Max.

Oh, God. She couldn't take Ruby home without Max seeing her.

"Why don't you think about this and call me tomorrow?" Stella said. "Please?"

Rachel shook her head, suddenly adamant in a way she didn't even recognize in herself. "I think this is the only way, Stella," she said. The words tumbled out without conscious thought, and yet rang truer than any others she could have spoken. "I never should have left her in the first place. It wasn't the right decision. Not for me."

"Under the circumstances..."

"The circumstances weren't her fault." Tears spilled slowly down Rachel's cheeks, and once they started, she wasn't sure they were ever going to stop. Except that Stella wouldn't even consider what Rachel was asking if she appeared to be falling apart on the outside as thoroughly as she was on the inside.

Brushing a finger beneath each eye, Rachel sat up straighter. "How soon can we set the process in motion?"

"What are we talking about here? A foster home until a family is approved?"

"If that's the way it needs to be for now, I'll go along with that, but only with the understanding that I be considered for the adoption."

"Rachel." Stella fell to the floor at Rachel's feet, kneeling with both of Rachel's hands in her own. "Please consider what you're saying. You have a fiancé who doesn't even know about any of this. How can you be certain he'll be agreeable to what you're suggesting?''

"I can't be," Rachel whispered. She couldn't even consider Max at the moment. If she did, she'd never go through with this. And if she didn't go through with this, she'd never be whole enough to marry Max someday if he'd still have her.

She couldn't abandon that child a second time. Not when the toddler was alone—more alone than her mother—and in so much need.

"I don't have all the answers, Stella," she said now, "but maybe I've been given a second chance here. Maybe the decision I made two years ago was the best one at the time. Lord knows, I was in no shape to be a parent, to raise a child. Especially considering the circumstances. But I'm stronger now, at least as far as facing Ruby is concerned. Parts of me may not be able to confront certain things in the past, but I'm ready to tackle the future. And maybe this is the way I meld who I was with who I've become. Maybe this is how I lay the past to rest—by finding what was good about it and embracing that.''

Stella held Rachel's gaze for a long moment, searching inside her, seeing the places Rachel had shown her at the darkest time of her life.

"It could take a couple of days to arrange for temporary placement. But it'll probably take less time than usual considering who you are.''

Rachel let out the breath she hadn't known she'd been holding. "Thank you," she whispered through a new sheen of tears.

"I can't make any promises." Stella stood up. "And I'm going to insist that you not see her until we know...."

"I understand."

"You also have to understand that even if you get temporary custody, adoption's not a certainty. Especially since you aren't married."

"I know. But it's a pretty sure thing that I'll get her, isn't it? Considering the circumstances?"

Stella turned away, busying herself with a folder on her desk.

"It's a pretty sure thing, isn't it?" Rachel persisted, standing behind her friend.

Whirling around, Stella said, "You have to be very certain about this, Rachel. It could backfire on you. Big time."

"It's a pretty sure thing, isn't it?"

Stella swore. "Yes, damn it, it probably is."

Moving in a body that was familiar, but with a person who was not, Rachel took the seat Stella indicated in front of her desk. Clearly and succinctly she answered all the questions Stella asked, signing forms that had to be signed. Giving permissions and verifications.

She even spoke with another counselor, one who was uninvolved and looking for signs that Rachel was not in full possession of her faculties. Other than her understandable problems dealing with the traumatic events that led to Ruby's birth, Rachel passed the preliminary examinations with flying colors.

In the space of a few short hours, she'd just set in motion the wheels that would irrevocably change her entire life.

She had no idea what she was going to do next.

RACHEL GAVE HIM hours to fall asleep. He still didn't succeed. Looking toward those glass doors with the offensive gold lettering for about the hundredth time, Max chomped back the urge to hit something. Hard.

His butt ached from sitting. He'd already taken a break outside to pace around the truck. And another one to walk down to the corner, thinking that surely by the time he got back, she'd be through. Though he'd kept his eye trained on that door so he wouldn't miss her—looking over his shoulder often as he walked— she'd never appeared.

Later, when his jeans were sticking to his thighs, damp with sweat from sitting in the cab in the hot sunshine, he'd chanced a trek around the block. But that had only brought disappointment when he'd finally rounded the last corner and she hadn't been standing there waiting by the truck for him. He'd even made a deal with himself. As soon as he quit waiting, she'd appear.

Yeah, right.

"Watched pots never boil," he muttered now, slouched down in the seat of the truck, his hat pulled over his brow in an effort to create a slightly nighttime effect. "Whoever came up with that idiocy?"

He'd kept his eyes away from the door for a full fifteen minutes. And it still hadn't cooked him up one Rachel Blair....

He jerked upright when the passenger door opened. She'd come out, walked around the truck, and he hadn't even noticed.

"I'm sorry it took so long," Rachel said, climbing up inside, closing the door quickly behind her.

"It's no problem," he said, assessing her. She was avoiding his eyes.

His stomach dropped. The day was going from not good to really not good.

"I'm here to help you," he reminded her. And himself, too.

She glanced at him briefly, the hair that he loved falling forward to veil her expression. "Still, it was horrible to make you wait like that. I had no idea I'd be so long."

"Don't worry about it. It's not like I had anything else to do." He didn't mind having waited now that she was back with him. He was glad he'd been able to do that for her.

He just wished he could do more. Wished she'd trust him with whatever was bothering her.

"Where to?" he asked now, his eyes on the rearview mirror as he put the truck in gear and pulled out into traffic. It wasn't one of the thousand questions he really wanted to ask.

"Back to the motel, I guess." She was gripping the strap of her purse so fiercely her knuckles were white. "Unless there's something you'd like to do."

Nope. Nothing. Except find out what in the hell was driving her.

"You found out all you needed to know about the Emersons, then?"

"Yes." She nodded, perhaps a little too vigorously. The knowledge obviously hadn't helped her demons any.

"And the baby?"

Rachel's head snapped around. "What about her?"

That was just it. He didn't know. Max ran his hand under the brim of his hat, feeling the sweat that had gathered there.

"I thought maybe you were in there looking for information on her. I didn't know if maybe you wanted to see her."

I don't know anything. And I'm afraid to ask you to share it with me. Afraid you'll fall apart on me and I won't know how to put you back together.

Rachel gave him the oddest look. Max couldn't decipher it. She appeared determined—and lost—at the same time.

She seemed as though she wanted to say something, but couldn't find the words. Or get them out.

He'd wait as long as it took.

Heading back toward the motel, Max tried to determine what to do next. Did they have an evening to kill before round three came in the morning? Or were they done in Austin? How in hell could he make a plan when he didn't know the mission?

Taking her mention of the motel to mean that they weren't leaving town just yet, he said, "Do you want to take in a movie? It's not even five o'clock yet, there's probably one starting soon."

She didn't say anything. Just sat there, staring vacantly out the front window. Her shoulders were bent beneath the weight she was carrying, and yet he had the feeling she bore it willingly. That she was determined to survive.

God, he loved her.

"A movie might take your mind off things for a bit and there's that new romantic comedy you wanted to see."

Still nothing.

If only he knew what was going through her mind. Knew what to say. Where they were headed.

Knew whether or not they were going to head there together.

He flipped the stereo on. And then back off again.

The music that usually calmed him was suddenly annoying.

"Max?"

"Yeah?"

"Can we go someplace and talk?" The words were soft, much more tentative than anything he was used to from her.

His heart started to beat a tattoo much like it had the one and only time he'd ridden rodeo and had been waiting in the chute for the door to open.

"Of course."

Rachel had still been in elementary school when he'd ridden in—and won—that rodeo.

"I...there's something I need to tell you. Something we need to talk about."

His mind scrambled, running through everything he knew about Austin, trying to figure out where to take her. She was ready to talk to him.

"I..." She paused. "We just need to talk. Before tomorrow."

His jaw tensed. *Before tomorrow.* That sounded ominous.

He was no longer sure he wanted to hear what she was thinking about. Just let him drive aimlessly around town, sweating and champing at the bit. Playing chauffeur for another few days.

Where was a ranch emergency or hand of cards when he needed one?

He pulled into a park they'd passed earlier that morning. Being a sunny spring afternoon, the swings were full and children and families were spilling out into most open areas with bikes and Rollerblades, picnics and kites.

Rachel stared at the goings-on in front of them, sending him a long searching look.

"Maybe we better go back to the motel," she said then, and his heart sank. She still didn't trust him enough to tell him what was wrong.

"I'd rather talk there," she added.

"That's fine with me," Max said, relieved that she was still planning to talk to him at all. He didn't care if she wanted to be on the moon as long as she'd finally confide in him.

Two days of stumbling around in the dark were taking their toll on his equilibrium.

Max felt a little awkward as he followed her into her room adjoining his. She dropped her purse on the dresser, turned on a couple of lights. And then a couple more.

Of their own accord, his eyes went straight to the king-size bed. And his loins responded.

What kind of disgusting jerk was he? Wanting to strip her naked and bury them both so deeply in that bed, in each other, that she'd forget whatever was ripping her up inside.

Did he really want her that way, anyway? Rachel was so much younger than him, their marriage was already at a disadvantage before they even began. The only way it was going to work was if she were absolutely certain—in her own mind and heart—that she wanted to tie herself to a man so much her senior.

She had to be absolutely certain. That was why he'd been trying so hard not to pressure her. Not to sleep with her and force her into a premature commitment for which she might not be ready.

"You want to order something to eat?" she asked.

She was standing by the desk, staring at a pamphlet on the motel's amenities.

It had a pool. HBO. A number to call for pizza. And a pretty decent complimentary continental breakfast. He'd read the card himself at least a dozen times the night before.

''Maybe in a bit,'' he answered slowly, his eye lighting on the ice bucket. ''A drink would be nice, though. How about I get us some ice? I picked up a small bottle of whiskey last night. One shot might do us both some good. Or I can get you a soda from the machine if you'd rather.''

Her eyes were filled with gratitude when she looked back over her shoulder at him and nodded. ''That would be great. Thanks.''

Max grabbed the bucket and escaped. For the next five minutes or so, he was a man with a mission. And a shot of whiskey waiting at the end of it.

It was a hell of a lot better than sitting in a baking truck waiting for his life to end.

RACHEL DIDN'T DRINK. He knew that. But for purely medicinal purposes, he encouraged her to have just one small nip when he got back to her room. Standing at the window, the cord to the blind wrapped around her hand, she looked as though she were ready to snap. She'd been staring out—through closed blinds.

Filling his glass with one healthy shot—all he ever allowed himself to have—he poured a splash of the amber liquid in another cup for Rachel. And then poured her soda over ice, as well, offering her both glasses at once.

She had to let go of the cord to take them.

Her hands were shaking so hard, Max's gut tight-

ened. How could he help her? How could he make this
easier for her when he didn't even know what "this"
was?

"I...this isn't easy," she said, setting the drinks on
the little round table in front of the window.

Max set his glass down as well, pulled out one of
the two upholstered chairs for her, and took the other
himself.

"Just throw it at me, whatever it is, as much as you
can get out," he said, forcing all the calm he could
muster into his voice. "We'll deal with it together."

It was the together part that he was hanging on to.

Her head slightly bowed, she looked up at him. "I
made a decision today." She stopped. Licked her lips.

He waited, when what he really wanted to do was
down in one gulp that shot of whiskey sitting on the
table in front of him.

"It's a decision that's going to affect the rest of my
life—our lives." She added the last with obvious dif-
ficulty. "If you still want us to have a life together
after all this is over."

Max heard "our lives." It was all he needed.

"Of course I want us to have a life together."

This wasn't about them, then. About her and him.
This running, searching, the pain. It wasn't about them.

Thank God.

Anything else he could deal with. No sweat. Bring
it on.

She looked straight at him, her eyes filled with so
many things he couldn't make them all out. But conviction was definitely one of them. And so much the
Rachel that he knew, he almost smiled.

"I'm going to adopt the Emerson baby girl."

CHAPTER SEVEN

THE SMILE Max had been holding back froze. His mind a total blank, he stared at her.

"Did you hear me?" she asked.

He thought he nodded, but couldn't be sure. He needed that shot of whiskey there in the water glass in front of him.

"When I was in the office today, I did the paperwork necessary to get temporary custody. I just have to wait for approval."

"Just like that."

"Mmm-hmm." Her eyes were apologetic as she nodded. She still hadn't looked away from him, holding his gaze steadily. And in those eyes he could see something he couldn't decipher—something that shut her out. Determination and a closed door, all mixed up together.

He didn't know what he'd been expecting. A story from her past, he guessed. Maybe he'd had a half-formed suspicion she'd been about to tell him about her affair with Emerson. Had spent a moment or two that afternoon wondering if she was still in love with the other man.

One thing was for certain: not once, even for a millisecond, had it dawned on him that she might be considering what she'd just said she was considering.

Breaking eye contact with her, he leaned down, both

elbows on his knees, and stared at yet another pattern on another motel room floor. This one was done in shades of beige and brown. In diamond shapes with flowered edges. Whoever heard of brown flowers?

"Say something, Max."

Brown used to be his favorite color.

Until now.

"What?" He couldn't think of anything. Felt out of place. Was floundering.

Didn't a couple usually plan an adoption together? Or at least mention it before it was a done deal?

What in hell had all that talk about her and him together been about? Didn't sound like she was planning on a *them* at all.

"Get mad. Tell me to go to hell. I don't know."

He didn't want to get mad.

"I know I should have talked to you first, Max. I know I should have, but the decision was made before I even knew it myself. This is just something I have to do."

"Regardless of how I feel about it."

"You are angry."

"No." He shook his head, his hands clasped lightly between his knees. "Just trying to understand."

"I...she...Max, I'm..." She broke off, and he could see he was losing her again. Her eyes were glazing, her breathing shallow and jerky. And then, as he watched, a change came over her. She shuddered and he could tell she was seeing him again. "I have no other choice."

"Even if it means we're through." He turned away.

"Are we through?" He couldn't look at her, but he could hear the sadness in her voice.

"I didn't say that," he told her, a sense of unreal

calm settling over him. Just get through this. That was all he had to do. Concentrate on what she needed. That was the way to do it. "I asked if going through this meant more than you and me, if it's something you're prepared to do even if it means you and I are no more."

She took too long to answer. He knew what she was going to say long before she did.

"Yes."

Max nodded. Sat up. Picked up his glass and emptied it. She watched him, her brow furrowed with what looked like pain—and worry.

"Why?" he asked, setting the glass down deliberately, sitting back, his hands on his thighs. It was a question he knew he shouldn't ask. She'd already tried to tell him—and failed. He'd seen it happen.

And yet, he had to ask.

He loved her. Everything else aside, he wanted to understand.

She glanced away, fiddled with the glass of whiskey he'd poured for her. "I—I have a debt to pay."

He had a feeling the words weren't the ones she'd been trying to say.

Frustrated, Max stood up, his chair tipping backward behind him. How could he help her get free from whatever was binding her all up inside? Waiting around, being patient, loving her didn't seem to be working.

"I'm sorry, Rachel, but I need a little more than that on this one." He cringed when he heard the tone of his voice, the words. The man who loved Rachel hadn't meant to say them. The one who'd been jilted on his wedding day, and at every turn since, meant them and more. "If, as you've implied, you still see us as a potential couple someday, as a...family—" he had a little trouble with the word ''—then you're going to have to give me something to go on here.''

Looking down at her, he wondered when he'd become such a jerk. Tears were spilling slowly from her eyes, dripping down her creamy soft cheeks. So much for tough love.

He knelt down in front of her, taking both of her hands in his. ''When did you stop trusting me, babe?'' The words were raspy. He needed another shot of that whiskey.

''Oh, Max.'' She ran one hand through his dark hair. ''I've never stopped trusting you.''

''You didn't trust me enough to come to me with whatever this is all about. Even now, with something as big as adopting somebody else's baby on the horizon, you won't trust me with the truth. You don't trust me to understand.''

''It's not a matter of trust.'' Her hand dropped into her lap. ''I have no doubt you'd understand.''

''What is it then?''

She tried to wipe away her tears, but they just kept trickling down. ''I...it's not...it's just...it's me, Max. I just can't talk about it. I'm trying.'' Her tears fell faster. ''Believe me, I'm trying so hard.

He knew she was. He could feel her trying. But if he could feel her so completely, why couldn't he fix whatever it was that was choking the life out of her?

''But you talked to whoever you saw in there today, didn't you?''

''I saw the caseworker. The name Dylan gave you. Stella Ramirez.''

''And did you discuss this thing you can't talk to me about?''

''Not really.'' On one level he was relieved to hear

that. So it wasn't just him… Rachel sniffled, then took a deep breath that turned into a sob. "I knew Stella before, Max. I met her in college. She knows things because she was around at the time, but the things I can't seem to tell you, I can't tell her, either."

He rubbed his face, looking for guidance, for some knowledge of what he was supposed to do. Because he sure as hell didn't know.

"Why?" he asked again.

"I've…because…I don't know…." She broke off. Shook her head. "It's just so dark and cold." She shivered, but Max didn't think she was even aware of it.

He stood, poured himself a second glass of whiskey. Took a sip. And waited.

He watched her slowly come back to herself, gather herself in, wrap herself up.

"There are some things about my time in Austin that are difficult for me," she finally said, sounding like a lost little girl—a ghost. Nothing like the very much alive woman he knew her to be. "I—I went to counseling before I came home. I honestly thought I'd dealt with them, put them behind me."

She'd gone to counseling. That was more information than he'd had since this whole thing started. Pertinent information. She'd needed counseling. This thing was bad. Really bad.

Max stood completely still, not wanting to move in case he'd startle her and she'd stop talking. She stopped anyway.

"What things, babe?" he asked softly, his heart going out to her. He was ready to take her pain away, if only he knew how. Knew where it stemmed from. Knew what they were discussing.

"I made some bad choices, and the consequences of those choices led to more bad choices."

She sounded like a sinner at confession. Remote, detached.

He sat on the side of the bed.

"I've been given a chance to do something, to maybe make amends."

"These choices, they had something to do with the Emersons?"

"One of the decisions, yes."

"And you think that by saving their child from state welfare you'll be able to atone for that choice."

"I don't know," she said, the raw pain in her eyes slicing through him. "I just know that I can't live with myself if I don't do this."

In a strange sort of way, he understood—even without the details. Feeling her need on so many levels, he searched for the right words to give her. And couldn't find them.

Max went to the bathroom, pulled the box of tissues from the silver metal dispenser and brought it in to her.

"I know this is grossly unfair," she finally said, her voice thick with emotion as she pulled a couple of tissues from the box. "I know it is and I hate myself for doing this, for not being able to just tell you. I keep trying but the words won't come out. I get dizzy and can't see and..." She started to get agitated again, her eyes darting around, her breathing coming in raspy jerks.

"It's okay, Rach," he said, though it wasn't at all. "It's okay."

It didn't take her as long to calm this time. He thought that was a good sign.

"Stella told me to keep trying," she said, her words still coming too quickly.

"Then we'll keep trying."

Her gaze lighted on him again, and Max was filled with a strange kind of warmth when he saw the gladness in her eyes as they focused on him.

"I—I have to find a way free, to tell you and still be able to live with myself afterward, you know?"

He didn't. But he nodded anyway because she seemed to need that. He had a feeling there was something very pertinent in what she'd just said. He had a feeling the answers he was seeking were hiding there.

"I don't blame you if you don't want to wait around while I get ahold of my life." She met his gaze head-on as she said the words, sincerity in the very depths of her eyes.

He met her gaze, hoping his own eyes were telling her the things his words should be saying.

"What are your immediate plans?" he asked, because he was still so much at a loss—and plans were the foundation of his life.

"To stay here for another day or two and see what happens with the temporary custody placement."

He nodded. "And then?"

"If it's successful, I'm going to take Ruby home...." Her words broke on a sob. One led to another, until she was crying so hard Max was frightened for her.

Then he did the only thing he knew to do. He lifted her out of her chair, into his arms, and sat with her on the bed, cradling her in his arms like the child he'd once thought her.

But she wasn't a child. She was a grown woman who was planning to take on a child of her own within the next forty-eight hours. Alone if she had to.

The testimony of her conviction spoke to Max, not in words, not even in ways he could understand, but it told him what he needed to know at that moment. He'd asked Rachel about trusting him, and now it was his turn to trust her. He had to trust her to know what she was doing. And to know what she could not do.

He held her for a long time, absorbing her sobs—and her pain—as much as he was humanly able. He didn't know if Rachel's pain was self-inflicted—if she was beating herself up over a mistake that she considered her fault—or if it had been inflicted upon her. He only knew what his job had to be now.

"Will you let me help you?" he asked when she was finally calm.

"Oh, Max," she whispered, her arms wrapping tightly around his neck for a second before she pulled back to look at him. "Are you sure you want to? This is all so unfair to you."

"Answer me this one thing, Rachel. Do you love me?"

"Oh, yes, I love you. I always have." There was no hesitation. No doubt.

His decision had been made.

"Then I'm sure I want to. We'll take that little girl home, babe. And when you're ready to talk, I'll be there to listen."

"Why?" It was her turn to frown. "I don't deserve this Max."

"Because I love you, too."

He'd finally found the words he'd needed to say.

VISIONS OF Julie's long blond hair and blue eyes accompanied Dylan Garrett as he made the trip down to San Antonio on Wednesday. Today was Julie's thirty-first birthday, and she was spending it away from all of her family and friends.

Dylan had been in love with Julie, with her porcelain skin and fiery temper, since his college days, and he wasn't going to be able to rest—or live with himself—until he eliminated the danger surrounding her. The danger that was holding her captive in a little town that wasn't home, where she had no family, where her past was unknown. She'd even had to take a new appearance. Brown contact lenses muddied her blue eyes, and her beautiful blond hair had been dyed and cut short.

And then there was little Thomas...

Switching his thoughts as he switched lanes on the highway, Dylan ran through the facts he'd unearthed so far, facts that incriminated his former best friend—and Julie's husband.

Sebastian involved with the mob? Dylan shook his head. He still couldn't quite believe it. Or believe that he'd been so completely duped. He was a cop—had been one hell of an undercover detective. And all the while, he'd been palling around with a professional criminal.

But no more. He was going to do whatever it took to find the evidence that would nail Sebastian for good. And to bring Julie and little Thomas home where they belonged.

Pulling onto Sebastian's street on the outlying reaches of San Antonio, Dylan took a quick professional glance around. Now that he knew of Sebastian's other life, Dylan was surprised by the lack of ostentatiousness in the single-story, stone-and-white stucco home.

Of course, inside the house was a different story.

Sebastian was waiting for Dylan in the large family

room—country music playing from the state-of-the-art entertainment system built into one wall. In the glass-enclosed dining area, he could see the table that Julie had always kept adorned with flowers. It was bare—not even a paper or two strewn about—looking like it hadn't been used in months.

"It was good of you to come down," Sebastian said, offering Dylan a drink in spite of the earliness of the hour.

It was barely three o'clock, and though he and Sebastian had instituted a practice in college never to drink before five o'clock, Dylan accepted the shot of whiskey.

"I couldn't let you do this day alone, man," he told Sebastian now, sipping a liquid so smooth it had to have been aged more than thirty years. It must have run Sebastian a couple of hundred bucks for that bottle. And there were more in the cupboard where he'd gotten it.

Sebastian studied Dylan under a furrowed brow for a moment and then looked away. "Right," he said. "Thanks."

"You hungry?" Dylan asked, standing there, glass in hand, feeling awkward in a place that had once been a second home to him. "We could head down to the sports bar...."

"I got some steaks to throw on the grill later," Sebastian said. "I didn't feel much like going out."

He flopped down onto one end of the couch, a big man, but looking suddenly smaller. His strong jaw—a Sebastian trademark with the women—didn't seem to jut out quite as much as usual.

Dylan had no idea what was on his friend's mind

these days. But Sebastian had once been in love with his beautiful wife. And this was her birthday.

Was there even one tiny regret? Any wish at all that his wife's life didn't have to be a casualty of his choices? He must know why Julie had really left, even if he would never confide in Dylan.

He settled onto the other end of the couch—his seat on all those Sunday afternoons when the two of them had spent hours of good-natured ribbing as they bet on the games they were watching.

"I remember when the two of you moved in here," he said now. "Julie made us rearrange this room six times before she was satisfied."

Sebastian looked around, his dark expression softening in a way Dylan hadn't seen in long time—and hadn't realized was missing until right now. "Yeah, but what other woman would have had an endless supply of homemade brownies to give the poor saps moving her in?"

"We should've been sick from eating 'em all."

"We worked it off."

"She'd made all those sandwiches, too. And had the cooler stocked with veggies and beer."

Julie was like that. Prepared. Aware. Always willing to go the extra mile. It was one of the things that made her such an exceptional journalist.

"I miss her," Sebastian said. Dressed in jeans and a polo shirt, the man looked little changed from their college days, when they'd been so comfortable with each other they'd strut around naked and neither one would care.

"I know," Dylan replied. And wondered if he missed Julie the person, or Julie who had something Sebastian wanted.

Finishing off his shot of whiskey, Sebastian gave Dylan a sideways glance. "No news to report?" he asked.

Dylan shook his head.

Technically, Dylan was still working for Sebastian. Allegedly trying to locate Julie, who'd been "missing" for more than a year. Dylan had found her months ago, but telling Sebastian would have jeopardized Julie's life. Sebastian was pretending not to know that Dylan was on to him, but Dylan knew he had suspicions.

So here they sat, both mourning the same woman. Pretending to still be part of a threesome they'd once thought nothing could ever separate. Dylan, Sebastian and Julie. They'd set out to conquer the world.

At least two of them had never counted on the mob, kidnappings, death and greed coming to play in their midst.

THEY HAD ANOTHER drink and caught up on the things that had happened in their lives since the wedding-that-wasn't on Saturday. At least the things that were happening on the surface of their lives. Dylan told Sebastian about Max finding Rachel, and the little vacation the two were taking. While Dylan grilled the steaks, Sebastian fixed a salad, heated a loaf of French bread and threw some potatoes in the oven. It was all very civilized, yet low-key enough to really be a day of mourning as they observed Julie's birthday without her.

And Dylan took every opportunity he had to find something in Sebastian's territory, something in the other man's manner, in his surroundings, his kitchen drawers and garage, that might implicate him once and for all.

Or at least give Dylan sufficient evidence to have

Sebastian put away long enough to find that vital link. And to be able to bring Julie home.

Through the entire meal, while he kept up his end of a conversation that just kept dancing around itself, Dylan was trying to figure out a way to get into Julie and Sebastian's bedroom. The house had two bedrooms, situated at opposite ends. One had been Dylan's whenever he'd stayed there, and he'd never had reason to venture down to the other end. No way could he casually decide to use the rest room in the master bedroom, when there was one in the guest room.

It was while Sebastian was on the phone, telling someone to check the files a third time for something that was missing, that it came to him.

"I'd like to take a look at Julie's things again," he told Sebastian as the two of them were finishing up in the kitchen.

Sebastian flipped the door of the dishwasher shut. "You're welcome to, of course, but I don't know what you expect to find. You've already seen everything there is to see."

"But maybe it's what we're not seeing that's the clue we're missing," he said. "We're so certain she left in a hurry, but what if we discover she did take something with her—something that might give us a clue where she'd been headed before she disappeared."

"Then let's go have a look."

Dylan followed Sebastian down the hall, a little disappointed at the easy capitulation. He'd hoped to put Sebastian on the spot, entering the other man's private quarters with no warning, no chance to hide anything that might incriminate him.

Dylan's scheme backfired on him. He didn't need to find any clues pertaining to Julie. He knew exactly where she was. And why she'd left. He'd even had an emergency connection to her twenty-four hours a day. But seeing all her clothes hanging there, thinking about the cheap, baggy things she was wearing these days, made him seethe.

Julie should be here, in her own home, with her own things.

God, he missed her.

With Sebastian watching over his shoulder, he got little chance to search the other man's things. He and Julie had separate closets in the master suite. Dylan had forgotten that. The top of Sebastian's nightstand was empty. There was nothing but cologne on his dresser.

With Julie's dresser top cluttered with her usual trinkets and pieces of jewelry, it looked as if the woman of the house were the person in residence. Sebastian had removed all of Julie's things from the main living area months ago, but he'd left them visible in here. Did that mean he still cared for his wife—at least some? That he perhaps found comfort in leaving their room as it had once been?

Thinking the entire day wasted, Dylan gave up. He might be trained to see more than most people, but it did no good if there was nothing to be found. He couldn't resist one more stop by Julie's dresser on his way out. Standing there looking at her things, he felt connected to her.

He remembered when she'd received that little white angel as a Christmas present from one of her sorority sisters in college. It had made Julie cry. Dylan had been pretty pissed when Sebastian had teased her about that. And there was the mock crystal hummingbird—Dylan had won that for her at a carnival in Mexico during a spring break jaunt the three of them had taken.

His eye passed over the china plate that held a couple of rings and several pairs of her favorite and less expensive earrings. And then came back. That earring there—the black one with gold filigree. He'd seen it before.

And not on Julie.

"You find something?" Sebastian asked, coming over to see what was holding Dylan's interest.

"Where'd that earring come from?" he asked.

"Don't ask me," Sebastian said. Dylan knew his friend had never understood Julie's passion for jewelry, but he'd encouraged her collection of some of the most valuable period pieces. There was no artist in Sebastian's soul, but his heart was all business. "She bought several pieces during our last trip to Europe."

"Mind if I take it with me?"

"No, but it's not going to tell you anything about her disappearance. They found that under the seat of my car last time I had it cleaned. No telling how long it'd been there."

Dylan had a sick feeling he knew just how long it had been there. If his suspicion was correct, that earring didn't belong to Julie at all.

He had to look at some pictures again, make certain that he wasn't losing his mind—a victim of desperately wishful thinking.

Heart pounding, Dylan pocketed the lone earring and took his departure as soon as he could get away without alerting Sebastian to his haste. His cell phone was at his ear before he'd left Sebastian's street.

"Lily?"

"Dylan? I thought you were at Sebastian's. What's up?"

"Get Diana Kincaid on the phone, arrange for a meeting between us as soon as possible."

"Of course," Lily said, obviously responding to the urgency she heard in her brother's voice. "It's not too late, I'll see if I can get her tonight. What do you need her for?"

"I think I've found the tie to Sebastian and the Kincaid kidnapping."

And that was the link that would put Sebastian behind bars forever.

CHAPTER EIGHT

THE CALL CAME Wednesday afternoon. Rachel had spoken with Stella on Tuesday and given her Max's cell phone number.

Rachel and Max were exploring The Drag—a famous old strip by the university. Guadalupe Street, which ran by the U, boasted everything from voodoo shops and tattoo parlors to bookshops and local restaurants. Max had never been there, so Rachel was sharing this bit of Austin flavor with him. When the phone rang, they were in one of her old haunts, a bookstore, browsing the shelves.

"Santana," Max answered on the first ring. Then, "Hang on, I'll get her."

He'd given her a moment's reprieve. Her heart was thundering so fiercely she could hardly breathe. His black eyes filled with understanding, Max handed the phone to her. And stayed by her side while she found the strength to say hello.

Right by her side. Where he'd been ever since their conversation in her motel room the night before last. No questions asked.

It was he who'd insisted on giving Stella the number to his cell phone, knowing that hanging out in a motel room was going to drive Rachel insane. And that to leave the phone—even for an hour or two—would do the same.

On Tuesday he'd offered to take her anywhere she wanted to go. Even shopping, which was something he detested. They'd ended up at a movie theater. They were both movie buffs, and since the closest theater to Trueblood was an hour away, being in a town with so many theaters and movies to choose from was like Christmas. It was also a great escape. They turned the ringer on Max's phone down to the lowest setting and sat way in the back so it wouldn't disturb the other moviegoers. So far they'd seen four movies.

And in between movies they walked. Residential streets, downtown streets, a mall. After the last movie, when Rachel was still too wired to sleep, he'd suggested a walk around the block where their motel was located. And then some of the neighboring blocks as well. When he'd tired her out to the point where she was laughing at something that wasn't funny at all, he'd dropped her at her door with a slow, deep kiss good-night. A kiss that had left her wanting more.

Not as much as he wanted, that was for sure. But at least...more.

Because of his steady, quiet strength, Rachel was able to get through the hideously long hours of waiting. She was also beginning to look back at the things she'd done. The person she'd been. Nothing was falling into place yet, but she was looking. It was a start.

Now, phone in hand, she walked outside the bookstore where reception would be better, and huddled in an alcove, away from all the people milling around. "Hello?"

"Rachel, it's Stella."

I know. "Hi." Seeing Max still inside the store, she motioned him to come join her. When he'd stood by her the other night, she'd promised herself she wasn't going to cut him out anymore. Not out of anything she could control.

"You've been holding out on me, woman. Who was that gorgeous-sounding man who answered the phone?"

"Max." She looked up at him. He *was* gorgeous. And kind. And far more than she deserved. "He's the fiancé I told you about."

"He's here in Austin with you?"

"Yeah."

"Was he here the other day, too?"

"Yes." *Tell me, Stella. Do I have her or don't I?*

"And does he know about Ruby yet?" Stella's voice had sobered. Pleasantries were over.

Rachel turned her back, studied a crack in the grout on the old brick building. "He knows I'm trying to adopt her."

"And he's agreeable to that?"

"Yes."

"Does he still intend to marry you?"

Looking around at Max, Rachel wished so desperately she could offer him the woman who'd been besotted with him before she left for college. "Are you asking as a friend or as a social worker?"

"Both."

She took a deep breath. It sounded like this was just a fact-finding call. She wasn't going to get an answer yet. The letdown made her weak. "We're still engaged."

Max didn't seem displeased by her pronouncement, but then he was concentrating on blocking her from the pedestrians passing by—affording her as much privacy as he could on the busy street.

"Have you set another date?"

"No." God, she hated this. Hated having her most personal thoughts and decisions open for public viewing. Even with Stella. She'd sworn after the last time that she'd never again be in a position to have to submit to such things.

And here she was. Staring at dirty grout, feeling invaded all over again. And knowing that Stella was right to be trespassing. Rachel hadn't finished healing yet. Or needing help, apparently.

"We'll need to know how permanent a place he'd have in Ruby's life, Rachel. He'd have to sign forms, undergo the same investigations we did with the Emersons."

She hadn't even thought about that—but she should have. She'd been through all of this before. How could she ask Max, quiet, keep-to-himself Max, to go through all of the interviews, the questions, the prodding into personal territory for a child who was nothing but a stranger to him? Especially without more of an explanation than she'd been able to give him so far.

She was going to have to do something to help herself. And soon. Maybe she should just keep forcing words to come until she passed out. And maybe each time, she'd get a little further, another word or two until he pieced them all together.

Light-headed, Rachel tried to find some kind of pleasing pattern in the dirty grout.

"Does it have to be done right now?" she finally asked, remembering the conversation she was having. "Even to get temporary custody?"

"No, but if you don't want to hold up adoption proceedings, it will have to be soon."

"I'll talk to him." Her stomach hurt just thinking about it. He hadn't signed on for any of this.

She wondered at what point he'd take his name off the dotted line—at what point he'd decide that tying himself to a besotted fool wasn't all it was cracked up to be and excuse himself from her life.

"I take it you still haven't been able to tell him?"

"No."

A cool May breeze blew across her skin and Rachel shuddered. She might be finding it impossible to make herself marry Max, but the thought of living her life without him was killing her.

"But you're trying?"

"Yes, constantly." She was a grown woman, she had to be able to speak of the horrors in her mind.

"Then you're doing all you can do, Rach, just don't give up. And in the meantime, I guess for now, everything's in order. Can you meet me at—" Stella rattled off an address on the outlying borders of Austin in a suburb that was neither nice, nor particularly bad "—at four this afternoon?"

Her heart started to pound, the phone slipping in her sweaty hand. That was only two hours from now. "Yes," she said, reaching up with her free hand to steady the phone. "Why?" She was afraid to hope.

And afraid to have her prayers answered, too.

She wasn't ready.

"Because that's the time Ruby's foster mother will be home and have her ready for you."

Sinking into the corner she'd been staring at for the past moments, Rachel gasped for air. "I got her."

Max turned and caught Rachel, holding her against him while she completed the call. And continued to hold her when she burst into tears.

THERE WAS THE TIME that wild stallion had found its way down to the Double G, running rampant throughout the corral, spooking every animal within a half-mile radius. A hundred head of cattle in the south pasture were threatening to stampede.

The stallion was hungry. Thirsty. There'd been a drought that year and all of the animals were a little more skittish than usual.

Without a flinch, Max had grabbed his rope, leaped onto his unsaddled, unbridled horse and lassoed the steed before any damage, other than to fences, had been done.

He'd delivered breech foals from testy mares, branded thousands of frightened animals. He'd survived droughts, tornadoes, a fire, and being thrown from his horse.

None of them had unnerved him like the drive to the less-than-stellar suburb of Austin that Wednesday afternoon. Rachel was a woman unknown to him, a land mine ready to explode at the least provocation with emotions he didn't understand. She sat stiffly beside him, staring straight ahead, tearing the tissue in her hands to shreds.

He was pretty sure she didn't even know she was doing it. The pieces were falling all around her.

"Would you like some music?" he asked, reaching for the radio.

"Sure. I don't care." She smiled, but there was nothing behind the expression, just a tilt of the lips.

Even in her agony she looked beautiful. A Madonna. Her creamy skin offset by the long red hair that followed its own rules, bouncing and waving all around her. She was wearing jeans again—a black pair that almost made Max jealous, the way they hugged her hips. And a short-sleeved sweater, the same shade of green as her eyes, outlined breasts that were perfection.

Shifting uncomfortably in his seat, Max was almost glad for the jeans that held his body's reaction to a minimum.

He glanced over at Rachel again. She was going to have one hell of a stiff neck if she didn't relax a bit.

"You think we got everything we're going to need for the next couple of days?" he asked. The back of his truck was filled with little-person paraphernalia. From clothes, diapers and cleaning things to jars of chunky-looking food and new toys.

"Yeah. Stella said the baby'll come with her own stuff anyway."

He nodded. That made sense.

He could hear Rachel's breathing when he pulled into the subdivision. Her right knee was bouncing up and down like a kid needing to relieve himself. He reached over and took her hand in his.

Her fingers were freezing.

"It's going to be fine, babe," he said, not completely certain why she was so agitated. Excited, he could see. After all, this was a huge step. Nervous even.

But something more than either of those emotions was coursing through Rachel. He could feel it. He just couldn't understand it.

She nodded jerkily, clutching his hand. With another quick look at her stricken face, he pulled her over next to him. She was drowning and he was her life preserver.

"How do you feel about all of this?" she asked suddenly.

"Me?" he glanced at her, then back at the road. Her

big green eyes had been steady on his as she nodded. She wasn't just making conversation.

"I don't know," he answered honestly. "I haven't really thought about it."

"She might become your daughter, too, Max." The words were soft. Tentative.

And hit him smack in the gut. His daughter. His and Rachel's.

It would take some getting used to. Where would he put a kid in his cabin? How would he keep it away from the big stone hearth that housed a fire for most of the winter?

And yet... "I'm ready to meet her," he said. And meant it.

He and Rachel. And a two-year-old. A family. Not quite the way he'd figured it, but doable just the same.

Yeah, he could get used to that idea.

He was almost grinning when he pulled into the drive of the neat, but in-need-of-a-paint-job house.

It looked like Rachel's friend Stella Ramirez was already there. She was talking to a woman in the doorway, presumably the foster mother.

"I'm scared." The whisper was barely audible.

"I am, too, a little," Max surprised himself by answering. "But you and me together, we can do this, Rach."

They could. He knew they could.

If only...

"RACHEL, how are you doing?"

The dark-complected woman who came out to the truck to meet them had to be Stella. Max liked the woman immediately, based simply on the compassionate understanding that shone from her eyes when she took Rachel's hand as Rachel stepped down from the truck.

"I don't know." Rachel laughed nervously in answer to the other woman's question. "I've got so much going on inside of me right now, I'm surprised my brain is still keeping the walking and talking part straight."

Stella hesitated. "Are you having doubts?"

"No!" Rachel was clearly very certain about that. "At least not about taking her, wanting her. Maybe about my ability to get this right."

Stella's face softened. "And there I have no doubts."

Max, having hung back, came around the front of the truck.

"Hello," he said, holding out one hand to Stella, putting his arm around Rachel with the other.

Giving his hand a firm shake, Stella said, "You must be Max."

"I am." He took off his hat and tossed it inside the truck through the door Rachel still hadn't closed.

"And are *you* ready for this?" Stella asked. Her astute glance was much more discerning than it had been when she'd looked at Rachel. He was being sized up.

"Yes, ma'am."

"If you two are going to be married anytime soon, we're going to need some information from you," the woman said, walking them slowly up the walk. "I'd appreciate it if you could stop by the office before heading back to Trueblood."

Rachel stiffened. Not knowing what that meant, Max said, "I'd prefer to come back next week, if that would work," he said. Maybe Rachel wanted to get right home with the baby.

And maybe she didn't want him going to the case-worker's office at all. Maybe a wedding anytime soon wasn't in her plans.

Frowning, Stella nodded. "Next week will be fine," she said, and then, taking Rachel's hand, she smiled. "Let's go meet Mrs. Butler, shall we?" she asked. "She's had Ruby for a couple of weeks now. She'll be able to tell you enough about her to get you started."

Enough to get started? And how were they supposed to find out the rest? He knew one hell of a lot about raising up calves and foals, but had a feeling that babies were a lot harder to raise than livestock.

Mrs. Butler was a tired looking, but kind enough woman. She had a couple of children of her own, both in school, and two foster children. They were all having a late-afternoon snack of cookies and milk and watching an educational show on television, she told them.

Max was relieved to hear that last bit. Television. He had one. And apparently this kid watched it.

"Have you got extra diapers?" the woman asked, blowing back a strand of her mousy brown hair. "I'm running short and don't have a car until my husband gets home. He's working late tonight."

She'd probably been pretty once.

"Yes," Rachel said, her voice sounding odd. Breathless. Higher than normal.

Max squeezed her shoulder. "We've got a full stock of supplies in the truck," he told the woman, including Stella in his smile.

"I wasn't sure what size she's in, so I got a couple of different ones," Rachel added.

"She's wearing twenty-four months in everything," Mrs. Butler said. "She's a small one, but remarkably good…"

Rachel stiffened again. Her tension transferred to Max. What in hell were they doing? Overnight, just like that, without plenty of thought and weeks to plan, they were standing there, ready to pick up the child of someone Rachel once knew, a child completely strange to both of them, and take her home.

How could they even play at being a family when they weren't a couple yet?

He started to sweat, wondering how to extricate them from the presence of these two women.

"You ready to go meet your daughter?" Mrs. Butler held her door open wider, smiling at Rachel through a sheen of tears. Surprised by the unexpected display of emotion, Max wondered why this woman put herself through fostering if it was this hard for her to lose a child.

He held on to Rachel. They didn't have to do this. If she needed to adopt a child to absolve herself from past sins—real or imaginary—then fine. But it didn't have to be this child. Didn't have to be now.

"I'm ready." Rachel stepped out of Max's embrace and through the screen door.

Because he didn't know what else to do, because he didn't want to leave Rachel to go through this alone, Max followed. The house smelled like laundry soap and tomato soup. It wasn't unpleasant, but still, they weren't two scents that went well together.

"She's right through here." Mrs. Butler's voice wavered as she pointed to an archway. "I'll go get her and bring her in." Before she left she pointed to some bags in the hall. "Those are her things, I've got them all packed."

Rachel nodded.

"Thank you," Max said.

Rachel stared after the woman, her neck straining toward the archway. He could hear the television in there, and some banging. But nothing else. Did almost-two-year-olds talk?

Stella was telling them that she'd called Mrs. Butler earlier that day so everything would be ready for them. And that she had a box of supplies for them out in her car.

Supplies were everywhere. What about the user's manual? Had anyone thought of that?

"Here she is!" The Butler woman's voice was filled with cheer as she returned—with a straight-faced, crumbs on the mouth, curly red-haired little girl in her arms. Max's heart jumped.

He didn't know much about kids, but if she were livestock he'd come to buy, he'd take her.

"Oh, baby." Rachel's eyes filled with tears as she reached out her arms. "Little Ruby."

Max moved behind her as she took the child from the other woman. "You're perfect," she said, smiling through her tears as she leaned back enough to see the little girl's face. She wiped the crumbs from Ruby's mouth. Touched the kid's cheek, ran a finger over her eyebrow and through her curls. "Just perfect."

Ruby studied Rachel, frowning, but Max figured she looked more like she was assessing Rachel than ready to burst a gasket.

She was a damn cute kid.

"She looks just like you," the Butler woman told Rachel.

Max thought it was nice of the woman to try to make Rachel feel a bit like a real mother instead of an adoptive one. And the kid did have red hair.

Smiling, still crying softly, Rachel looked up from

the precious cargo in her arms. "You really think so?" she asked. And then hugged the baby.

Ruby looked at Max over Rachel's shoulder, frowning at him.

Max wondered if he should frown back.

She had green eyes. Familiar-looking eyes. Where had he seen eyes like those before?

Mrs. Butler sniffled, pulled a tissue out of the pocket of her blouse. "I'm sorry," she said. "I don't usually go all mushy, but I've never heard of this before and it's so great."

Stella stepped forward as if to forestall the woman.

Never heard of this? How could a foster mother not have heard of her charges being adopted? Or was it that she never met the prospective parents herself?

Rachel was so filled with the child in her arms she didn't even appear to be there with the rest of them.

"I mean, to be able to give a baby back to her birth mother…"

What?

"No!" Stella's cry was background noise.

The Butler woman thought they were someone else. Was this even the right kid?

Max intercepted a look between Stella and Rachel. He couldn't see Rachel's expression, but Stella's definitely said she was sorry.

And worried.

Max backed up a step. What in hell was going on here?

Was he the only one who was confused?

Ruby squirmed, her tiny face screwed up into a ball as she pushed against Rachel.

"Sorry, baby," he heard Rachel murmur, her voice

choking on a sob. "Mommy didn't mean to squeeze so tight."

Ruby poked a finger into one of the tears resting on Rachel's cheek. "Schee?"

"What?" Rachel asked, focusing completely on the child.

"Schee?"

"I think she's saying 'see', but I'm not completely sure," Mrs. Butler said. "She says it a lot, and not always when it makes sense."

Birth mother. Max couldn't get beyond those two words. He was certain he'd heard them.

They couldn't be right, and no one was doing anything to correct them.

"You just called Rachel Ruby's birth mother," he heard himself say. His face felt stiff, like he'd been riding in the cold for hours. "You must be thinking of somebody else. Rachel's never had a child."

The three women exchanged a look that scared Max. He met Rachel's eyes, not sure what he was reading there. Not sure he wanted to know. "Tell her, babe," he said.

Ruby pointed a wet finger at him. "Schee?"

He stared at the child.

"She's right, Max." Rachel's words came from far off—and had an odd sound of relief laced through them.

The red hair. Those familiar green eyes.

Max's blood turned cold.

CHAPTER NINE

RACHEL WAS TEMPTED to walk home. She didn't want to separate her body from Ruby's to put the baby in her car seat. Didn't want to have to let go of her at all.

But she owed it to Max to get in that truck with him. To give him as much of an explanation as she could, even though she knew it wasn't going to take the frozen look off his face. He was probably stricken. Certainly disappointed, shocked. But he was a private man. There was no way he'd ever let the two women standing there watching their dramatic byplay know how this was affecting him.

With final goodbyes out of the way, the curious glances and concerned good wishes behind them, Max loaded Ruby's things into the back of the truck while Rachel belted the baby's car seat onto the bench between her and Max and then strapped the little girl in.

"She doesn't seem to be the least bit disturbed about going with us," she said when Max climbed silently in beside them.

He took a good long look at the child. Rachel wished so badly she could see into his mind, know what he was thinking.

He was going to make such an incredible father someday.

Tears sprang to her eyes as she thought of the possibility of Ruby missing out on that.

"I suspect she's been passed around enough the past few months to take it in stride," was all he said before starting the truck.

Rachel pulled a couple of toys from the diaper bag Mrs. Butler had handed her and gave them to Ruby. The baby took them—one in each hand—studied them, dropped one and started pushing the buttons on the one she held. A little clown face popped up.

"Schee?" The little girl grinned.

Rachel's heart shattered into a million pieces. It might not be Ruby's first smile, but it was *hers*. She'd missed so much.

Max turned onto the highway and Rachel had never been more aware of his big, steady strength, his large hands clenching the wheel, guiding them safely along.

"I'm sorry," she said softly. Her gaze left her daughter to take in his rigid jaw. His black eyes were focused on the road in front of him, and he was steering with both hands.

She thought he hadn't heard her. She was going to have to tell him again. But then he nodded.

There was so much she needed to say to him, though some of it she still couldn't even think about. His knowing about Ruby freed her of at least some of the guilt.

Some things she was going to *have* to tell him now. But how much could she say in front of her little girl? How much could a two-year-old understand?

She glanced back at Ruby, her heart filling with a love she couldn't even comprehend. Ruby's eyes were drooping, her face half-covered by the blanket she'd picked up from the side of the car seat where Rachel had carefully, tearfully set it.

It had come with Ruby from the Emersons, and Mrs.

Butler said the child never went anywhere without it. Though it was very worn, Rachel recognized that blanket. She'd bought it during her last week of pregnancy. The only thing she'd left with her illegitimate, unwanted child. Besides a huge piece of her heart.

"I'm sorry I couldn't tell you myself." She spoke softly, not wanting to disturb Ruby. But also because she was feeling calmer suddenly.

Something had fallen into place for her this afternoon. She'd righted a terrible wrong. Not a moral wrong, but a sin against herself.

Did she dare hope that meant other sins might be righted someday?

Her father would certainly say so. But then, he still had faith.

She was dreading telling him about this secret—the child she'd borne in shame. She worried what effect the entire situation was going to have on his faith in the Almighty they'd both served so diligently all their lives. The God who'd deserted her in her greatest hour of need not once, but twice. Her father had had a hard time forgiving God the first time, much harder than she had. She didn't know how he'd handle the news of the second.

But one thing she did know, her father would love Ruby. And the two of them deserved to know each other, to share that love.

She'd always known that.

"Why couldn't you tell me?" Max's question startled her, it had been so long in coming.

"A lot of reasons." Rachel spoke slowly, thinking, searching her heart and mind for the true answer to his question. "Partly, because I didn't want you to think less of me."

That was the easiest one.

He didn't comment.

She wished she knew what he was thinking of her right then. How far would she have to travel to regain any of his regard? If she could regain any of it.

Max was a fair man. And she hadn't treated him fairly.

"The main reason, though, was because it was just too painful to talk about," she told him. And the words, once they started to flow, just kept coming. "I agonized so much over giving her up, Max. It went against everything I felt, everything I believed, everything I wanted. But at the same time, I didn't want her. I had no way to support her, no life of my own yet, let alone a life to offer to someone else, though I don't think I would have let that stop me. But there were some... circumstances...around her birth that made it impossible for me to keep her."

Max nodded, as though he somehow knew what those circumstances were.

He couldn't know. There was no possible way for him to know. But it was somehow a relief to have him think he'd figured it all out. It let Rachel off the hook.

If, by some miracle, their relationship progressed, she might someday be able to tell Max about that time in her life. Right now, she couldn't even think about it without getting dizzy with panic.

"Anyway," she continued, concentrating on the things that she could deal with, "after I finally made the decision to give her up, I couldn't look back or it would destroy me. I did what I had to do. I interviewed family after family, spent months reading files and medical reports looking for the people who could give her the perfect home—and ended up right back where

I started. With the Emersons. I'd been so certain at first that I didn't want to go with them, because they were both so involved with their careers, but they'd been the only right choice all along.''

Max drove silently. One hand left the wheel, coming to rest on the bench beside the car seat. He'd put his hat on when they'd come back out to the truck. It rested low on his forehead, partially concealing his expression from her. His gaze never left the road.

''After that, I didn't let myself think anymore. I just went through the motions of staying alive until it was all over.…'' She stopped when her voice broke. She might be stronger that afternoon, but there were still many raw wounds that she carried. That she might very well carry for the rest of her life.

A woman couldn't give away a baby that had grown inside her body, that she'd nourished and cared for in the most intimate ways, without losing a part of herself in the process.

And while she had Ruby back, at least temporarily, there were so many things she'd lost that she'd never be able to reclaim. Her daughter's entire babyhood. All of those important firsts.

In all the ways that mattered, she hadn't even been Ruby's first mother.

''Afterward,'' she continued after a time, finding enough calm in the Texas landscape rolling past to finish what she'd started, ''the only way I could survive was to let her go. Completely. Because I chose an adoption that allowed my involvement, I had the right to monthly reports on the baby for the first year, accompanied by photos.''

She swallowed. She couldn't look either at Max or the child sleeping peacefully, blessedly, beside her.

"The first month, when the envelope came, I could hardly bear to touch it. It sat in my mailbox for three days—until just knowing it was there was driving me insane. I took it out and made myself read what was in it. I thought it was a part of my penance—the price I had to pay for the mistakes I'd made."

"The preacher's kid." Max's words surprised her. They'd been spoken with a strange kind of affection—not the sarcasm she deserved.

She glanced at him, and her stomach leaped at the compassion she saw mixed with the other emotions in his gaze.

"I couldn't eat after that," she said slowly, trying not to remember too clearly as she continued her story. "I never had morning sickness when I was pregnant, but after that letter came, everything I ate made me sick. I ended up losing over fifteen pounds. I started to get light-headed when I stood up, tiring fast. I knew I was in trouble and called Stella. I ended up in the hospital—and counseling—before it was all over."

"You did the full counseling?"

Rachel tensed, her internal danger signals ringing. "Yes."

"Good."

Good. The word was comforting somehow.

"By the time I was able to go to classes again, I knew that I couldn't look back anymore. The only way I was going to get over the past and have any kind of future at all was to walk completely away. I told Stella I didn't want any more reports. I finished school as quickly as I could, and I came home."

"Leaving everything that happened behind in Austin."

She nodded. "I'd already given her up, Max. What

good would it have done to bring her memory home when all it would bring was pain to innocent people?''

"We might have been able to help you through it.''

"There was nothing anyone could have done that you didn't already do. In my mind, she no longer existed.''

"Apparently she did,'' he said quietly.

A couple of tears dripped slowly down Rachel's cheeks. "That was in my heart.''

His hand moved over, almost touching Ruby's little white laced-up shoe. Rachel longed for bits of Max's steady reassurance herself.

"You'd changed when you came back.''

"I grew up.''

"Maybe,'' he said, frowning, pushing his hat back on his head. "That's what I told myself, but I sensed more. I'm sorry I didn't listen to my instincts and try harder to find you in there, Rach.''

Fresh tears sprang to her eyes. They'd been falling inside her for two long years.

He was sorry.

"I'm sorry I made such a mess of my life. And now yours. And probably Daddy's, too.''

"Your father doesn't know?''

She shook her head. And then, realizing his eyes were on the road, she said a quiet "No.'' But he knew some things that Max didn't. Things the hospital had told him when they'd called him. Things that were going to make Ruby's existence so much harder for him to bear.

Max drove silently for a while as dusk started to fall around them. Ruby slept on, the sound of her steady breathing an incredible joy to Rachel. A comfort and a reprieve.

"I think we should take her to my cabin tonight," Max said some miles down the road.

Her mind in other places, trying to figure out how she could have done everything differently, Rachel needed a second to figure out what he was talking about.

And to realize the impact of what he was saying.

"It'll be late by the time we get home—especially if we stop for dinner. I assume she's going to need to eat when she wakes up since she was only having a snack back there. And I think this isn't something we should throw on either her or your father when everyone's tired."

She agreed. Her father would have a much better chance of weathering the news if they caught him on a sunny morning when he was rested rather than in the dark of the night. But...

"You don't have to do this, Max," she said. "I'm not going to hold you to any promises. I never intended to. This is my mistake, my problem."

Sliding around the end of the car seat, his hand grabbed her own, his gaze leaving the road long enough to collide with hers. "If we're ever going to have a chance, the first thing you've got to do is learn to trust me."

"I do tr—"

"No, you don't." He shook his head. "Or at least not enough. Marriage is for better or worse, babe, and that's what I was ready to sign on for."

"You're saying that today, finding out that I'm not the innocent preacher's kid you thought me to be, doesn't change things?"

"Of course it changes things. How could it not?"

He glanced at Ruby.

Licking her lips, Rachel took a deep breath. "Changes them how much?"

It scared her that his answer mattered so much. She had to be strong. She had a daughter to think about now.

"I don't know," he said. "I'd like to know more about what happened. Obviously my image of you has altered in some ways. It's going to take a little time to get used to the fact that you're actually a mother...."

He sent her a lopsided attempt at a grin, and for the first time since she'd run out on her wedding, Rachel felt a fleeting sense of peace.

"You've lost a lot of respect for me, haven't you?" she asked, figuring it would be better to just get that right out in the open since she was so aware of it. Losing his respect made her bone-deep sad.

His thumb rubbed back and forth across the top of her hand. "I haven't lost any respect for you."

"I have an illegitimate child," she said softly. As horrible as the words sounded, they also brought freedom. She was no longer having to hide from herself. Hide herself from everyone else. At least where Ruby was concerned.

"You think you're the only one who makes mistakes?"

"No, but—"

"I'm hoping you're going to tell me what happened when you're ready," he interrupted. "Until then, I have to go on what I know, Rach, and I know you. You wouldn't have landed in this position unless the circumstances were extreme."

Tears sprang to her eyes. "Thank you."

She could barely see his nod in the falling dusk. "I

really admire you for what you're doing here," he said. "With her."

"You do?"

His head turned toward her. "I do."

And with that, Rachel would be satisfied.

WITH THE Trueblood water tower just a mile or so up ahead, Max automatically reached for the phone to call the Garretts to let them know he was back. Everything about Trueblood was familiar to him. The smell. The sights. The cracks in the road and the shapes of the trees whizzing by in the dark. It felt good to be home. To be in well-known territory, where he was in control.

The baby next to him whimpered in her sleep. Max put the phone back in its cubby in the dash.

He couldn't tell the Garretts he was home. Not tonight. Not with Ruby in tow. Reverend Blair had the right to be the first to know. And Rachel had a right to a good night's sleep before she tackled that hurdle.

"You're sure you want us at your place tonight?" Rachel's voice broke the silence that had fallen between them for the last ten miles or so. He'd just taken the turnoff for the Garrett spread.

"Of course."

Max glanced sideways as a truck passed them, the headlights showing him Rachel's expression. She was tense again, ready to spring.

"She might cry in the night, keep you up."

"I don't need a lot of sleep."

"But what if she breaks something?"

He was more worried about something breaking her. "If you don't want to come to the cabin, babe, just say so."

"Oh!" she turned to face him. "No!" She stopped.

"I mean, yes, of course I do, I just hate to put you out more...."

"Rachel," he said, his voice sterner than he could ever remember using with her. "Either we're in this together, or we're not. Decide now." He couldn't help her if she wouldn't let him.

"Together." Max almost smiled when the answer came so quickly. But another thought just occurred to him.

"Are you worried how it's going to look, you staying alone there with me?" They weren't in Austin anymore.

"Not hardly." She chuckled. The sound did something to Max's insides that he wasn't used to. She glanced at her sleeping daughter. "It's a little late for that, wouldn't you say?"

He couldn't argue with her there. Trueblood was a small town. An old-fashioned town. And she was the preacher's daughter. She had some tough days ahead.

Days he would bear with her right by her side—if she didn't push him away again. It wasn't something he'd ever worried about before. Wasn't anything he ever wanted to worry about again.

Problem was, with Rachel he just couldn't be sure anymore.

CHAPTER TEN

HE'D FORGOTTEN that he'd prepared the cabin for his new bride. He'd had Lily bring in a dried flower arrangement the day before the wedding and set it on the plank wood table in his dining alcove. There was a bucket with a bottle of champagne and two glasses beside the flowers, just waiting for the ice. And the couple who were supposed to be popping the cork.

There were new cream-colored sheets on the king-size bed upstairs as well. His and her towels in the bathroom upstairs. And a couple of magazines he'd seen Rachel read on the coffee table in the living room, compliments of Lily.

Damn.

"You've made some changes," Rachel said, coming in behind him.

He turned, a sleeping Ruby lying across his shoulder. "Just got rid of some of the old horseshoes."

"A lifetime's collection of them," she said, a warm smile lighting her tired features. "I hope you kept them."

"You can't tell me you really want them up in your living room."

"No," she said, looking around slowly. "But maybe in that office we were going to add on for you."

"I saved them." He had one from every horse he'd

ever owned. And from most of those he'd broken as well.

"Good."

Rachel set her purse and Ruby's bag down in one of the overstuffed brown armchairs that looked great in the home of a rugged man like Max. And very strange with a baby's diaper bag in the center of it.

She turned around slowly, and then again, her gaze alighting on—and avoiding—the champagne.

"She sure is a heavy sleeper," she said, her voice not quite steady.

He grunted. He supposed she was, but it was past the baby's seven o'clock bedtime. What else would she be doing, but sleeping? "We've got that portable crib thing out in the truck. I'll bring that in and set it up upstairs. You can have my—"

"No!" She stopped, looked down, her hands clenched in front of her. And then she looked back up at him, her gaze clear. "I'm not going to take your bed from you, Max." When he started to protest, she forestalled him. "Don't argue with me or try to convince me why it would be best because I don't care. I'm not doing it."

Max grinned. "I was merely going to say that it probably made more sense for you to take the guest room upstairs as all of my things are in my room and yours are still out in the truck and a bit more mobile."

"Oh." She grinned back. "Okay then." Their eyes met, and had he not had a sleeping baby against his chest, Max would have damned caution and hauled her into his arms.

God, she was beautiful. And he'd been waiting for what seemed two lifetimes too long to taste the fullness of her sweet skin.

"Um..." Rachel looked away, licked her lips. "Would you like me to take her, or go get the stuff from the truck?"

"Take her." He practically shoved the baby at her. He would have offered her some food to eat while he was busy, except that they'd stopped for dinner an hour before so she wouldn't be hungry. Ruby had woken up long enough to finish off two jars of some kind of mush stuff, but she'd fallen back to sleep the second they'd put her back in the truck.

Besides, Max couldn't offer her any food. He didn't think there was much. A couple of cans of beans. A frozen burrito or two. A box of stale cereal, maybe. He'd been planning to dine on Rachel his first night home and had completely forgotten to go to the grocery before he'd left. Probably because he never went to the grocery.

Until now, he'd taken his meals up at the ranch house.

By the time he had the truck unloaded, Rachel was settled in the spare bedroom upstairs. She'd changed the baby into some pajamas with feet in them and was sitting in the old wooden rocker Max had inherited from his mother and father. Ruby was awake but drowsy, seemingly content to snuggle against Rachel's breast and drink the bottle Rachel had prepared for her out of some powdered junk and a bit of water—a more portable concoction than milk, she'd explained, because it didn't have to be refrigerated.

He unfolded the baby's bed thing with one pull and dropped the thin little mattress inside. "Sure hope her appetite changes soon," he muttered.

"What?"

"That stuff she eats. It's going to change to steak

and potatoes soon, right? And real milk? We're raising cattle here, for cripe's sake.''

''They're beef cattle, Max.''

As quickly as he could, Max brought up the rest of the things Rachel would need for the night, careful not to take another look at her, sitting in his mother's chair with a baby at her breast.

The sight had raised such an instant and completely unexpected yearning inside him that he knew it was time for him to make his exit. Take a look around his own small holding—the tiny ranch adjacent to the Garretts' that had been bequeathed to one of Max's ancestors from some Garrett long ago.

''I'm right across the hall if you need anything,'' he told her after his last trip up.

''Thanks,'' Rachel said. Her voice sounded far away, as though she hardly knew he was there. Max looked over at her once, briefly, and bolted.

There'd been tears rolling slowly down Rachel's cheeks as, head bent, she studied every inch of the baby she'd given birth to but never really seen.

And as strongly as he'd felt compelled to go to her, to help her through the difficult moments, he felt more strongly compelled to leave her alone.

Making peace with her baby was something Rachel was going to have to do alone.

With a heavy heart, he left the female Blairs alone.

SEBASTIAN COOPER shoved his foot to the floor, pushing his wickedly expensive sports car to the maximum of its high-powered eight-cylinder engine. He knew right where he was going, looked forward to the challenge of the winding roads ahead. There weren't enough curves in Texas to stop him. He could master them all.

His phone rang and, letting up on the gas only slightly, he handled the powerful machine with one hand as he picked up.

"Cooper."

The voice on the other end was the one he'd been waiting for.

He listened. And then swore.

The message was not what he'd been expecting to hear.

"Hattie Devereaux is one damned peon black woman," he growled. "Find her or I'll find someone who will. I told you before—find her or you're done. The clock's ticking."

Punching the off button, he tossed the phone onto the seat beside him and sped up into the next curve....

RACHEL WASN'T SURE if she slept at all. Certainly not more than a quick doze if she had. The night passed in such a strange blend of miseries and joy, of memories and lost hopes, of dreams and wishes come true that she wasn't certain if she'd actually lost consciousness or merely escaped into the recesses of her mind.

She heard Max come in downstairs sometime after midnight. She hadn't even known that he'd left the house.

But she knew when he was back. Heard every move he made. The champagne cork as it popped. And later, the bottle as he set it down on the table. And then again. He must have gone from pouring the bubbly liquid into a glass to drinking straight from the bottle.

Lying in the double bed she'd had to make up earlier that evening, she felt every muscle in her body tense when she heard his heavy steps on the stairs. They passed his door and came down to hers. Her heart was beating so rapidly she could hardly breathe.

And then the steps retreated. Quietly. As quiet as the man himself. Leaving Rachel feeling small and alone in the bed that hadn't been intended for her use at all.

She spent the rest of the night tuning in to the uneven cadences of Ruby's breathing as she dreamed the dreams of the helpless and innocent. When the dark hours grew into endless tunnels of torture for Rachel, she turned to the only other thing she knew, the good Lord her father had taught her about.

"God," she whispered, first in her mind, and then, just in case, aloud. She slipped out of the bed and down to her knees, a place she hadn't been in years. "God, I don't know if you can hear me," she started. And then stopped.

What was the point?

There was no God watching over her. All the good works in the world hadn't been enough to earn her his protection.

And where did she go from there?

"But..." She squeezed her eyes shut hard, trying to find Him, but all she saw was stars. "If you're there, I'm related to Reverend Donald Blair. You know him, I think." Delirious with exhaustion, besieged by conflicting emotions, she rambled, reverting back to the child she'd been the last time she'd tried this. The night before she'd gone to the party that had changed her life. "Anyway, I'm not asking for anything for myself, but could you please protect Ruby because I don't know the first thing about being a mother. And Max, too? I don't know what to do about Max, or know why I love him so much when..." She broke off, a tear sliding through her tightly shut eyes. She'd thought she was all cried out. "And Daddy," she started up again. "Let him know you're there, God. Speak to him tomorrow when I tell him..."

She might have fallen asleep there on her knees. Rachel wasn't sure. But it was almost half an hour later before she finally climbed back into bed. Nothing had changed.

The demons were still raging within her.

But her stomach was a little calmer as she lay there and waited for daybreak, listening to her daughter breathe and wishing she was in the strong, comforting arms of the man lying just across the hall.

SHE CALLED her father while Max was in the shower the next morning. Ruby was on the floor at her feet, cheerfully ripping up a magazine she'd found on the coffee table. Because it was a women's magazine—and not one Max was likely to be interested in—Rachel let her. It was keeping her happy. And quiet.

"Rachel, baby, where are you, girl?"

"I..." She looked around Max's kitchen, his mail on the counter, the coffee cup he'd used that morning on the rack in the sink. "I'm going to be in Trueblood later this morning and I need to talk to you, Daddy," she said. She might be a grown woman, but she was still her father's daughter. The one he'd raised lovingly and single-handedly. "Are you going to be around?"

"Of course, I'll make sure I am," he said immediately. "You want to meet me at the house?"

He was usually in his office at the church on weekday mornings, but with Ruby...

"Yes, if that's okay?"

"What time you want me there?"

Rachel named the hour, giving herself just enough time to shower when Max was finished and get into Trueblood. Her nerves weren't going to last much longer than that.

"Fine," Donald Blair said. And then, "You all right, Rachel girl?"

"Yes."

"Is Max still with you?"

"Yes."

"Good," he said. The relief in his voice brought a fresh spate of tears to her eyes. He wasn't going to be feeling nearly so good soon. In about an hour, his entire world was going to come crumbling down around him.

Not just because Rachel had a child he knew nothing about, but because it was going to be very hard for him to accept that the Fates could be so cruel.

Backing up from the phone, Rachel fought the urge to run again. There was going to be no more of that. Period.

And yet, it broke her heart to think of putting her father through the crisis of faith Ruby's existence had started in her. She'd gone to the hospital. They'd done a D and C so that a pregnancy wouldn't result from the incident.

And a month later, she'd found out she was pregnant.

There'd been some sperm still in her vaginal canal, they supposed, or maybe it had traveled up higher, to her fallopian tube. In any case, it had remained behind in her body and found an egg.

How could God have let something so terrible happen to someone like her? And to a good man of the cloth like her father?

When it had been merely unsolicited sperm they

were cleaning out of her body—a routine medical procedure after certain violent acts—the hospital's recommendation had seemed right to her. But once that sperm had found an egg, once a life was growing inside her, the baby actually made, she hadn't been able to contemplate the abortion they'd encouraged her to have.

"Schee?" Ruby's tiny voice stopped Rachel short. The little girl walked toward Rachel on unsteady feet, a tiny, colorful corner ripped from the magazine clutched in her outstretched hand.

"Schee?" she said, holding it up to Rachel.

"Yes, darling, I see," Rachel said, picking the baby up and holding her close to her heart.

She couldn't blame God for this. She couldn't blame anyone.

Not when her heart was so filled with thanks.

THE WATER SLUICED down Max's body, vibrating against the highly sensitized nerve endings of his skin. Being under the same roof with Rachel was testing his self-control more than he'd have thought. Damn. It wasn't right that a guy had to walk around with a land mine sitting inside him.

Water off, he dried himself quickly, vigorously, steering his mind to other matters. What he needed to do was get back out on the ranch. His own small spread as well as the Garretts' much larger one. Working the land was what he knew, what he did well. What he was completely certain he could do.

Child rearing was not.

Though, so far, Max figured he might be able to handle having little Ruby around. The kid came with more pounds of stuff than Max weighed, and he'd had to carry it all—out to the truck, in from the truck, upstairs, downstairs. But that was all he'd had to do.

He'd yet to hear the baby cry.

She'd eaten more mush for breakfast—letting Rachel feed her without complaint. And then she'd taken another one of those powdery bottle concoctions. Those things were going to have to go.

The clean diapers kept disappearing, to be replaced by wrapped-up soiled ones. He'd carried them out to the trash. More carrying.

Nothing he couldn't handle.

As a matter of fact, he thought as he buttoned up his denim shirt and tucked it inside the waist of his jeans, if what he'd seen so far was what it took to raise a kid, he had it down pat.

Now if only he could get the mother part right....

ASHLEY HAD ARRANGED to have a couple of ranch hands retrieve Rachel's car from the dealership after it had been serviced, but until they'd spoken to Reverend Blair, Max didn't want anyone to know they were back.

The ten-mile drive to the rectory was a tense one. Even little Ruby seemed to sense the unease in the air. She started to whine for the first time since they'd taken custody of her.

"What, punkin?" Rachel asked softly, handing the little girl her prized blanket. "You shouldn't be hungry, you just had a snack before we left."

With imploring, big green eyes, Ruby glanced at her mother, over at Max, and back again. Dividing his gaze between the little girl and the road, Max got a bit nervous.

If the kid couldn't tell them what was wrong, how in hell were they going to get her to stop? And how much time did they have until the whine turned into the full-scale squalling he'd been unpleasantly exposed to in restaurants from time to time?

"Look at this, Ruby!" Rachel said, holding up the toy that the baby had been so happy to play with the day before. Ruby pushed it away. Her lower lip was jutting out, trembling, her tiny chin one big dimple.

Damn. Max started to sweat. It was coming. The full-blown wail was coming. And while he may know squat about kids, even he could figure out that it was going to be a lot harder to get the kid to quit if she got herself worked up.

"Try that bah bah thing Mrs. Butler told us about," he said, pulling his hat down a little farther on his forehead. Too bad the damn thing didn't reach over his ears.

"I don't believe in them," Rachel said. "They aren't good for teeth and are habit-forming. I don't want to make her too dependent."

For a day-old mother, she sure had a lot of set ideas. "Mrs. Butler said that she likes her bah bah sometimes. The way she used Ruby's words to describe it so you'd know when she was asking for it made it seem pretty damn important."

He had no idea what the damn thing even was. He'd been busy stacking the things he was going to carry in the truck when the foster mother had gone through Ruby's diaper bag with Rachel. All he knew was that the bah bah was in that bag. And Ruby liked it.

"I don't—"

How much could one time with the bah bah, which had apparently been made for babies, hurt the kid's teeth? Especially since she only had six? He and Rachel had counted them when they'd stopped for dinner the night before. There were only six.

"Rachel," he interrupted, "please try it. If you don't want to continue with it, then fine, but it's probably best to keep things as familiar for her as possible right now, and if that thing is familiar…"

Rachel frowned. "You're right, Max." She reached in the bag. "I should have thought of that."

A piece of rubber nipple appeared. Ah, a pacifier. Max was a bit relieved. He knew what that was for.

As soon as she saw what was in Rachel's hand, Ruby strained toward it, her little bird lips closing around the funny-shaped plastic nipple as soon as it was within reach. She was immediately quiet.

Max relaxed in his seat.

THE REVEREND Donald Blair was an imposing man. To his parishioners he was the eye and the voice of God. To Max Santana, he was the father of the woman Max intended to bed.

Either way, he was not a man who was easily approached with difficult news. He came out into the yard to greet them as soon as he heard Max's truck.

"You okay?" Max sent Rachel a long, reassuring glance as he put the truck in park and turned off the key.

She nodded, her gaze darting, wide-eyed, to the father she adored. "Do you think he sees her?"

Ruby spit out her pacifier and leaned forward, reaching for the toy she'd pushed away earlier.

"Let's go meet your grandpa, little girl," Rachel said, unhooking the car seat strap and pulling Ruby onto her lap. She adjusted the pink velour pants and pink-and-white blouse the baby was wearing, pushing the wayward, curly red hair back from her little forehead.

"Let me carry her," Max heard himself say, reaching for Ruby.

Rachel let her go reluctantly, took a deep breath, and got out of the truck. Max followed right behind her, the toddler held firmly in his arms.

"Schee?" Ruby said, poking her finger up his nose.

"That's a nose," Max said. "And you don't normally touch them." The kid had a lot to learn.

But she had someone to meet first.

"Rachel, Max…" Donald's ready greeting froze on his lips. "What's going on?" he said, staring at the baby in Max's arms.

The minister looked like he'd seen a ghost.

"Daddy, this is Ruby," Rachel said, her voice trembling. Her eyes were moist, but she didn't let any tears fall.

Max swallowed. He'd do anything to make the next moments easier on her. He just didn't know what could be done.

"She's a great kid, sir," he said. "She has six teeth, eats like any new filly should, and likes magazines."

Pale, his features tight, Donald stood there staring. His gaze moved slowly from Ruby to Rachel and back again.

"You have something you need to tell me, Rachel?" he asked, his penetrating gaze on the little girl who pulled two fingers from her mouth and tried to shove them into Max's.

Rachel nodded, not that her father could see her. "She's mine."

"I can see that," Donald said, still staring at the child.

Rachel's father showed no reaction at all. Not anger. Not rejection. And not the unconditional love Max had heard him preach about, either. He just kept staring.

And looking far too tired for so early in the day.

"I'm sorry, Daddy," Rachel said, the tears finally spilling over. She didn't back down, his brave and strong fiancée on the run. Just stood there hurting for her father, waiting.

"No," Donald said, and then, as though he'd just been turned on, he sprang around to his daughter. Pulling Rachel into his arms, he buried his face against her hair. "Don't you ever be sorry, Rachel girl. Not for this. Never for this."

Max was surprised to see tears in the other man's eyes.

"But…"

"Shh," Donald said, releasing his grip on his daughter only enough to place one finger against her lips. "I know."

Suddenly, Max was a bystander. Rachel and her father were having a mostly silent conversation in a language he'd never learned.

Donald turned to look again at the child Max was still holding. Ruby was busy with the top button on Max's shirt, her slobbery fingers slipping inside the shirt to the chest hair beneath as she tried to pull the button free from the cloth.

"She looks exactly like you did at that age," he said softly. "It's like going back in time."

"I'm glad." Rachel gave a teary smile.

"It's right," Donald said. "The child not looking like *him*."

"Daddy." Rachel's voice held a very distinct warning and was accompanied by a look in Max's direction.

"Oh," Donald said, instantly understanding something that Max didn't get at all. A look passed between the two of them—something that definitely translated to Max as, *We'll talk later.* Rachel was watching her father closely, her brow creased with what looked like a mixture of concern and fear.

Odd, while Donald had known nothing about the child Rachel had borne, he apparently knew about the affair that had led to the child's birth. Max wanted that piece of information. Badly.

He was fairly certain the father was Emerson. It made sense. Rachel would have been horrified to have found herself involved with a married man. It even made sense that the Emersons would have been the last couple she'd want to give her baby to, and yet, in the end, the most perfect. But what Max wanted to know was how a woman as conscientious as Rachel ended up having unprotected sex.

He was certain there was an answer.

He just hadn't found it yet.

"So," Donald was saying, approaching Max, "how about if you let an old grandpa see his little girl?" His voice, though slightly forced, was light and welcoming.

Ruby went straight to the older man, studying his face as thoroughly as she'd studied Rachel's and Max's the day before.

"She's sure a friendly little thing," Donald observed.

"We think it comes from living with so many different families in so short a time," Rachel said, joining her father. She held one of Ruby's hands in hers for a second.

"Why so many different families?"

"Her adopted parents were killed on New Year's

Eve,'' Rachel revealed without much of the pain Max knew she had to be feeling. ''She's been in temporary care since then, until a more permanent placement could be found.''

She filled Donald in on the past couple of days only briefly as they stood out in the yard, entertaining Ruby with the big cross hanging from her grandfather's neck. Max knew there would be much more discussion to come. Donald wasn't asking any of the questions that had to be raging through his mind. Max wondered if his reticence was because of the little girl he held, or because of Max.

Rachel told Donald how Max had helped her with her search, that he'd been there every step of the way. He'd even guessed right about the pacifier on the drive out.

Idiotically, that last bit restored a measure of the confidence Max was quickly losing as he stood watching the two of them.

''I can't thank you enough, son,'' Donald said, his gaze still perusing his first grandchild.

He seemed delighted with what he saw.

And that, more than anything, validated what Max had already known himself. Whatever had happened in Austin had not been something frivolous or immoral. Without one word, Rachel's father was in her camp, as accepting—if not as needy—of the child as Rachel had been.

They kept exchanging looks over the toddler's curly red head. One thing was very clear to Max. Something had bound the two of them irrevocably together.

And it was something they weren't sharing with Max.

CHAPTER ELEVEN

"WE'LL SET UP the spare bedroom as a nursery." Donald Blair was sitting on the floor of the living room at the rectory, handing his granddaughter toys out of the bag his daughter had brought.

Rachel smiled at him, shocked at how easily he'd come to accept Ruby's existence. She and her father had had a moment alone in the kitchen—one where they spoke volumes without the words Rachel had never been able to give her father. So far his faith seemed to be amazingly intact.

And then she heard what he'd just said. Set up the nursery. There.

Rachel frowned.

Ruby walked over to take a ball with shapes from her grandfather. "We can move the furniture out to the garage," Donald said.

"I don't think that's a good idea, Daddy." She was sitting in her father's recliner. Max was standing over by the window, where he'd just distracted Ruby from banging a big plastic rattle against the pane.

"It would be easier than converting your room."

"I don't think it's a good idea to move Ruby in here."

She wasn't sure where she was going to go. An apartment in Trueblood, she hoped. She just knew that she couldn't come back home.

Donald looked up, his hand suspended in midair holding a baby doll. "Of course it's a good idea."

"People will talk, Daddy."

"The talk's not going to change if you move out."

"Yes, it will." Rachel nodded. She was going to be firm on this one. She knew it was right. "If I'm here, then you've sanctioned what's happened...."

Donald started to interrupt and Rachel forestalled him. "Let me finish, please?"

Ruby came up and snatched the doll out of Donald's hand. He looked at her as if he'd forgotten about the toy he'd been holding, then bowed his head.

"Continue."

"The truth of the matter is, I have a child out of wedlock. That's considered immoral around here."

"But—"

"You said I could finish, Daddy, then I'll listen." She looked up at Max. He nodded, but said nothing. She sure wished she knew what he was thinking. "Some of your parishioners hold pretty black-and-white views on life, Daddy, and they look to you for the guidance that keeps their lives on an even keel. In a world as crazy as this one, they need you for that stability. They'll never be able to view Ruby with an open mind, and because of that, they won't be able to understand you openly condoning her existence in such a supportive way as to have her live here. They wouldn't be able to come to church knowing that she was living in the rectory."

"That's their problem," Donald interrupted harshly. Ruby handed him the doll, minus her hair. He took it—and the hair—and put her back together. "Jesus' teachings are exactly the opposite—"

"I know that, and so do you, but not everyone sees

things that way. And if I'm living someplace else, you'll be able to please everyone. Those who are too small-minded to accept and forgive a mistake will be satisfied that you're not condoning my behavior by having me live in your home. You'll still be able to be supportive, to love Ruby and be a real grandfather to her—because that would be the Christian way—without jeopardizing the souls of some of your most devout members.''

"I will not have them dictating to me how I care for my own flesh and blood.''

"You are a man of the cloth, Daddy, you owe your life to these people. You've told me that often enough. This rectory is theirs, not ours.''

"Then we'll move.''

"No!'' Rachel stood up, followed Ruby as she headed over to the coffee table. She was afraid the little girl was going to topple forward and hit her head. "You won't move. You're too important here, Daddy. Your work is too important. You really help these people. You show them week after week how to take their daily lives and find more joys than sorrow. You can't stop doing that because of me. Most especially not because of me. Please don't add that to my list of things to be sorry about.''

Leaning back against the couch, Donald held out his arms as Ruby planted her diapered bottom on his lap to read a plastic book she'd just picked up. Helping her turn the pages, he asked, "And have I done that for you, daughter? Have I taught you how to find the joy?''

Sharing another glance with Max, who'd been silently attentive to the entire conversation, Rachel told her father, "I'm learning.''

Silence fell for a moment while Ruby babbled a make-believe fable from the pictures she was studying. And then Max came forward, sat down on the edge of the couch, his forearms propped on spread knees.

"I haven't spoken to Rachel about this yet, sir, and probably should have first, but I'd like her and Ruby to stay at my place."

Shocked, Rachel stared at him, unable to speak. Her crazy heart was beating way too fast with far too much joy, considering the circumstances.

"You two aren't married yet," Donald reminded Max quietly. They couldn't ask Rachel's father to accept such a liaison.

"I'm hoping to remedy that soon," Max said, "if and when Rachel's ready." He sent her a long glance, making the statement a promise. "We're still engaged," he added.

Donald looked at both of them. "You've officially decided that?" he asked. Rachel nodded.

"We've discussed it," Max said. "But for now, Rachel would share the spare bedroom at the cabin with Ruby. If she even wants to come at all."

Rachel's eyes met his, and again she felt a return to the closeness they'd shared before she'd blown everything. "I do."

"Rachel's going through a tough time," Max said, his voice quiet, but sure. "It's my right to stand behind her, to support her completely. People are going to be talking about her anyway—why not let her have another backbone to take some of the sting?"

He'd do that for her. He had to really love her to do that for her. Rachel wanted so badly to be whatever Max needed her to be. Except that, other than a sex partner, she had no idea what that might be. The man was as self-sufficient as they came.

"Your reputation will be shot," Donald said, but Rachel saw that her father was giving the idea serious consideration.

"I've never cared what people think about me." Max handed Ruby another book. "But even if I did, I figure at least this way, in their eyes, I get the girl. The other way has me playing the poor old groom who was left at the altar by the beautiful young bride."

"I'm so sorry," Rachel told them both. "I've made such a mess of things and that's just what I've been trying to avoid for more than two years."

"You've made the absolute best you could out of a horrendous tragedy," Donald said sternly. "Let us love you, girl. It's the only thing we actually have the power to do."

She chuckled, but filed her father's words away to pull out later. She had a feeling that she would need them.

"Another thing to consider," Max said slowly, looking at Rachel from beneath his brow, "is Ruby." He picked up his hat from where he'd thrown it on the corner of the couch when they'd come in, and started working on the brim.

Her heart went out to the big strong man who was suddenly having a hard time controlling all that life was throwing him. She'd never seen him look so vulnerable.

In that moment, before she even knew what he was about to say, Rachel fell in love with Max all over again. Not the love of the pubescent teenager, or even the love of the disillusioned young woman, but the mature kind of love that would see her into eternity.

"If all goes as planned, I'm going to be her parent, too. I think it's best for her, most fair to her, to let her get started on the stable family unit she's been denied the past few months. I may not know much about child rearing, but I know that the more you move living things around, the less rooted they become."

"He's right, Daddy. Ruby and I belong with him."

She'd been speaking to her father, but Rachel was looking straight at Max, promising him more than she'd been able to promise him that morning. Or any of the past few mornings. She didn't know if she'd ever be over her past, if she'd ever be able to be the wife he deserved, but for as long as he'd have her, she was going to stand beside him, doing whatever she could to share his life and make him happy.

"You two are going to do this, whether I approve or not," Donald said. He didn't sound angry, but rather was merely confirming a fact.

Max looked back at Rachel, receiving her message, though she wasn't sure he knew for certain what it meant.

"We'd like your approval, though," he said, breaking eye contact with Rachel as he spoke to her father.

"How long you going to make me wait before you set a wedding date?" he asked.

Max glanced her way, leaving that one solely up to her. Without warning the walls closed in again, dark walls, sliding up on both sides of her, squeezing her until she was aware of almost nothing but their blackness.

But from somewhere inside her, there was more than just darkness. There was the knowledge she'd gained over the past couple of days, the assurance that Max loved her. That she was stronger than she thought she was. That she loved Max more than life itself.

"Is next week okay?" She heard the words echo from far away, too busy fighting off the panic to notice Max's frown.

"Next week is fine," Donald said. "I'll have the church ladies get everything back on. The cake. The flowers. Everything just like it was. Your mother would have wanted that."

He didn't seem to notice that he was the only one of the three adults present who was feeling any joy.

DYLAN AND LILY were sharing the sandwich Lily had brought upstairs with her for lunch. She'd come into Dylan's office looking for some information that she needed, and lost half her sandwich in the bargain.

Sitting down across from him, Lily wasn't in any hurry to leave. She had a load of work to do, yet nothing that couldn't wait until she found out what was behind the tired look on her brother's face.

"Still nothing on Sebastian?" she asked, knowing that what lay most heavily on her little brother's heart was Julie. She only hoped that once Dylan solved this case—and he would solve it, Dylan was the best—Julie would finally realize that he was the man she should have chosen all along and put her brother out of his misery.

Chomping the last of her tuna sandwich, he shook his head. "But I know if I can just reach Diana Kincaid, she's going to identify that earring and through it Sebastian as the man who kidnapped her."

Lily looked again at the earring that had been sitting on the corner of Dylan's desk since he'd brought it home from Sebastian's. She looked at the picture underneath it, too. The one taken of Diana when she'd been rescued. Her hair was a mess, her clothes ripped. And she was wearing only one earring. It wasn't completely identifiable, but from where she was sitting, Lily had to agree with Dylan. The two earrings looked like a match.

"What a time for her to pick to go out on the road," Dylan said, then swore a blue streak.

"Politicians don't get to schedule political campaigns around their own schedule," Lily reminded him dryly. "And Diane wants to see her dad reelected governor."

She hoped, for all their sakes—but most of all Dylan's—that they reached Diana soon. That she'd be back in San Antonio and able to identify her missing earring.

She'd seen Sebastian at Max and Rachel's wedding. The man had been a tiger with his prey in sight. She had a feeling Julie's time was running out.

"I think Max is back," she said now, remembering she'd wanted to tell Dylan that, but also wanting to get her brother's mind on something besides Julie for at least a moment or two. "I saw his truck when I was coming over a little while ago."

Though his body was still slumped in his tipped-back chair, Dylan's gaze perked up. "Was he alone?"

"No." Lily frowned. "It was the strangest thing. Rachel was with him, but it looked like there was someone else in the truck, too."

"Anyone we know?"

"Not hardly. Whoever it was was in a car seat. And maybe a year or two old."

Dylan's chair came down with a thunk.

"I'll be damned."

"What?" Her brother knew something she didn't.

"The Emerson baby," Dylan said, explaining absolutely nothing at all.

And the look on his face, that closed, it's-not-mine-to-tell look, told her that she wasn't going to get an explanation, either.

Damn. She hated that.

RUBY FELL ASLEEP on the way home from the rectory. Wordlessly Max carried her upstairs to her portable crib, laying her down and covering her as he'd seen Rachel do the night before. Ruby didn't even seem to notice.

The kid was amazing. She went a hundred miles an hour while she was awake, needing constant stimulation, and apparently was just as serious about her sleep. He was hoping there were a lot of sleeping parts to her day. Otherwise he and Rachel were going to need marathon running shoes—for their brains.

"You can fill those with whatever pleases you," he said, coming back downstairs to find her looking through the predominantly bare kitchen cupboards.

She opened another empty cupboard. "It looks like you haven't been shopping since we went together at Christmas time."

It was shortly after that time that Max had quit bringing her to the cabin. On New Year's Eve he'd barely stopped himself from taking her to his bed, and he'd refused to tempt himself a second time.

"You know I don't particularly like to cook, and since there's a full-time cook up at the ranch, there didn't seem to be much point in filling cupboards." Not without her there.

"I'll go to the grocery today." Opening the drawer

by the phone, she grabbed a pad and paper and started making a list. Keeping a little too purposefully busy was Max's determination.

He leaned back against the counter, his arms crossed at his chest, and frowned. "Mind telling me why you told your father we were getting married next week?"

Faltering, Rachel had to try twice to put back the box of stale cereal she'd just checked the date on. "Because he asked." She turned, facing him.

She looked like she was squaring off for a duel, which was fine with him.

"You asked me to live here," she reminded him. "You told him we were still planning on getting married. I thought you meant it."

"I did."

"Then why be mad about it?"

"I'm not mad."

"You look it," she said. "You sound it, too."

"I'm not mad."

"So—" she lowered her lashes and then raised them again, "what are you?" Her voice had grown softer, needier, touching Max in ways he didn't get touched.

"I'm wondering why you think you're going to be any more able to marry me next week than you were last week. I'm wondering why you told your father you'd marry me so soon when the look in your eyes said it was the last thing you wanted."

Rachel glanced away. "For Ruby?" Her gaze turned back toward him.

"Try again."

She didn't need to marry him for Ruby. They both knew that. Rachel was perfectly capable of raising that baby by herself. She'd been prepared to do just that. He'd been an afterthought.

She looked around the kitchen, down at her feet, over his shoulder, anywhere but at him. And when her gaze finally did land on his, her eyes were filled with emotions he couldn't decipher.

"I don't know, Max," she said.

He believed her.

"I want to marry you so badly," she continued, giving him the honesty he'd been looking for. "I've wanted to be your wife for more than half my life."

The cords in his neck relaxed as he waited for her to go on, to finish the 'but' he heard at the end of her sentence.

"I'm ready to live here, to share your life with you," she said. She leaned back against the counter directly opposite him, her ankles crossed, arms folded tightly against her chest.

Max loved seeing her there. Hearing her there. In his private place. His real life.

"These past couple of days showed me very clearly just how much I'm meant to be with you. Even in the toughest of times, being with you completes me."

Max was having a hard time just standing there. He had to fight the urge to pull her up against him and complete her in ways he'd never completed her before. Ironically enough, considering the words she was saying, he had the distinct feeling that to touch her right then would be the worst thing he could do.

The messages were so mixed he wasn't certain he was getting either of them entirely correct.

"It's just that..." She sighed and looked up at him with pleading green eyes, invoking a silent vow from Max to give her whatever it was she needed. "I've got to take care of these things—inside me—and until I do,

I'm scared." Those last words came out in such a rush, he knew she'd been holding them in a long time.

"Scared of what?"

"Getting too...close...to anyone."

"Anyone, or just me?"

Her eyes grew wide. "Anyone—in that way." She said that last as though he'd know exactly what she was talking about.

Max didn't. But remembering the glazed, darting eyes and uneven breathing she'd been attacked with every time she'd tried to explain things to him these past few days, he was reluctant to pressure her. This had to happen in her time, when her psyche was ready to deal with whatever she had to tell him. He knew about Ruby, and she was the most important piece of missing information. For now, as long as it wasn't *him* Rachel had a problem with, he didn't have a problem, either.

"So why have your father plan the wedding for next week?" he asked, coming back to his original question.

"Because I think we should get married." Her gaze was a little unsure as she watched him. "That is, if you still want to."

"You think forcing the issue is going to make you more capable of dealing with whatever is holding you back?"

"Running from it wasn't the answer."

"And what if marriage isn't, either?"

"I know I want to marry you."

"You didn't know that last weekend?"

"Not like I know it now."

Max nodded, gratified by that answer. "And what if, after we say 'I do,' you're still not ready?"

"Then we take it one day at a time until I am."

He could live with that. It was kind of like being on the outside looking in on his own marriage. But he could definitely live with that.

CHAPTER TWELVE

MAX DECIDED to go to work that afternoon. After having him to herself for so many days, Rachel was kind of sad to hear that. And maybe just a tad afraid to be left alone with Ruby. What if the little girl needed something and Rachel couldn't figure out what it was?

What if she did something that made Ruby not like her?

"I'll be back in time to drive into San Antonio for dinner and to pick up a real crib and whatever else you need," he said, standing at the door to the cabin. "If you'd like to, that is."

Walking toward him, Rachel smiled. "Of course I'd like to. Thank you." She stopped just short of him, gazing up at his tall good looks, loving him. "Once we adopt Ruby I'd like to keep all the money the Emersons left for her in a trust fund and just pay for everything she needs. Do you mind?"

She'd given this a lot of thought. But now that she was marrying Max again for sure, she was going to have to consider his wishes as well. She had enough money of her own to cover the upcoming expenses, but Max was going to be Ruby's father. He should have a say...

"I wouldn't have it any other way," he said, his eyes gentle as they gazed down at her. "I just assumed, since we paid for the stuff in Austin, that that was how you wanted it done.''

"I wish they hadn't sold so many of Ruby's belongings in the settlement of the estate." Rachel frowned. "It would have been nice for her to have the things the Emersons picked out for her."

"I can see the new family wanting to make her their own," Max said. "To decorate her room the way they wanted it."

Decorate her room. Rachel was going to be decorating a nursery, not just imagining someone else doing it. This had all happened so fast, and there were so many things she hadn't had time to consider yet.

She'd known she had to have her daughter. There'd been no doubt. And no time to consider all the ramifications. Besides, no matter what they were, she still would have brought Ruby home.

She was going to get to decorate her daughter's nursery. To pick out a crib. And sheets. Curtains, and a little dresser. Fabrics and colors that would go with Max's rocking chair.

Filled with sweet anticipation, she was suddenly looking forward to the afternoon. The planning...

"I don't know where I'm going to be," Max was saying. "I'm heading up to the ranch house now, to see Dylan, and then out to check on the boys. But I'll have my cell phone if you need me."

Rachel chuckled. "Just go," she said. "We'll be fine."

"Yeah." His brow furrowed as he looked at her. "You will be."

With his hat in his hands, he stood there looking at her for another second, and then, before Rachel could read his intent, he pulled her into his arms.

His lips on hers were hot and urgent. His tongue probed her mouth, coaxing her to open up to him. Without conscious thought, Rachel did just that, exploring him just as he was exploring her. Exchanging passion for passion. Desire for desire. He was the best kisser she'd ever known. Confident. Sure. Giving.

He groaned, grinding his hips against hers, much more demanding than he'd ever been in the past—more hungry than he'd ever let her see.

His kiss forgotten, Rachel started to tremble, the old familiar feeling coming back to swamp her. Anytime he got too close, anytime he made her completely aware of the manhood pulsing to get inside her, the darkness returned.

Pretending that nothing had changed, she concentrated on returning his kisses, on absorbing his groans, welcoming his passion. How could she love a man so much—want him so badly—and be so frightened of him at the same time?

"I'll see you later," he finally said, breaking the kiss to run one finger down her cheek. He was staring at her lips. "If I don't go now, I might not go at all."

His voice was husky. Out of breath.

Rachel's heart was beating hard, too.

With one last quick kiss on her lips, he was out the door. Gone.

Rachel held on to that last kiss, to the pleasure his kiss aroused in her and the need for so much more.

She tried to forget about what had happened when he let her know he wanted more, too.

Somehow she was going to get through this. Somehow she was going to find a way to be Max's wife.

There was no other option.

THE FIRST THING Rachel did after Max left—besides running upstairs to check on Ruby, who was still sound asleep—was call the Isabella Trueblood Memorial Library.

Debbie Anderson, her fellow librarian and good friend, answered the phone. She was alone in the library, but only while the librarian from San Antonio who was covering for Rachel was out picking up take-out food for them both. Though Rachel had worked briefly in San Antonio, she didn't know the other librarian.

"Where are you?" was Debbie's first question when she heard Rachel's voice.

"Back in town." Rachel paused. "Out at Max's."

"I was worried about you."

"I know." Rachel wrapped the phone cord around her index finger. "I'm sorry."

"Don't apologize!" Debbie said. "I know you well enough to know you had a damn good reason for skipping town. You were insanely in love with Max. There had to be something pretty big to chase you off."

Rachel smiled, warmed by Debbie's unconditional support, and also by her respect. Debbie wasn't going to ask.

"I'll have to go into explanations later," Rachel said, fingering the button on her jeans. Much later. "But I had some unresolved issues in Austin. A baby I'd given up for adoption." Rachel didn't know how else to break the news except to just say it.

"What?" Debbie asked. "I thought I heard you say you had a baby." The two had been friends for a couple of years before Rachel went away to college. From the time Debbie had come to Trueblood, barely graduated from college herself, to take over at the True-blood library.

"I did. My junior year of college. She's just over eighteen months now."

"She? You really had a baby?" Debbie's voice would have been squeaking if she hadn't had such a husky tone to begin with.

Rachel studied the cracks between the planks of Max's hardwood floor. Whoever laid the floor had been very precise. "I gave her up for adoption."

Rubbing the back of her neck, she tried not to let the walls close in on her. Over the past day or two she'd thought a bit about showing up in town with an almost two-year-old baby, but she hadn't prepared any specific explanations.

Now she was wishing she had.

Debbie still wasn't asking any questions. Rachel loved her for that.

"I found out a couple of days ago that her adoptive parents were killed in a car accident and Ruby was living in her second, soon-to-be third foster home. It took a couple of days, but Max and I went and got her and brought her home. We're adopting her ourselves."

"Wow."

Rachel figured Debbie's statement just about covered it.

"Yeah." Rachel tried to chuckle. "So right now, I'm wondering how well the temporary librarian from San Antonio is working out."

Rachel wasn't due back at the library until Monday, since she was still technically on her honeymoon, but she was hoping not to have to go back at all. At least not in the immediate future.

Max had already told her that he'd be perfectly

happy not to have her work unless she wanted to. He'd been telling her that for a couple of months. He was financially sound enough for neither of them to have to work. Of course, he'd never give up his job as foreman of the Double G. And she hadn't been able to imagine herself not being around the books she loved while he was gone all day.

But that was before she'd found something that she loved far more.

Ruby.

"Great, actually," Debbie said. "Renee's going through a divorce, no kids thankfully, and is really enjoying the small-town, friendly feel of Trueblood. Rather than commuting from San Antonio like she'd planned, one of the five rooms at the motel was open and she's been staying there. I have a feeling she'd be thrilled to take us on full-time."

"Will you ask her for me? That is, if it's okay with you."

"Of course. She's gone to lunch, but I'll ask as soon as she gets back."

"Thanks, Deb," she said softly. She didn't know what she'd done to deserve such faithfully loving people in her life.

"No problem. But hey," she added when Rachel would have rung off. "When do I get to meet this darling of yours?"

"Soon," Rachel promised. "Maybe today. I'm hoping to get into town to buy some groceries. Max's cupboards are more bare than Mother Hubbard's."

"You're living out there?"

"Yeah."

"And your father knows?"

"Yeah. Daddy's been great."

"Wow."

"Max and I are getting married next Saturday. You'll be there, won't you?"

"Of course."

"I haven't even called Ashley yet," Rachel said, remembering her matron of honor and best friend. Life had been so crazy the past several days, and she'd had so much on her mind. "She had my car picked up for me as we'd originally planned, but she doesn't know about any of this."

"She will soon," Debbie said, chuckling. "This is Trueblood and word travels fast here."

"I know." Rachel was both thankful for that, and dreading it. The shock of her unconventional return would be over more quickly. But facing all the reactions at once would be much more intense.

"You know I won't say anything."

"Of course I know that. You're the best, Deb."

"I know," Debbie teased. And then, more seriously, she asked, "Does she look like you?"

"Looking at pictures of me when I was her age, she could be me," Rachel said.

Debbie didn't ask any more, and Rachel didn't offer anything about the other contributor to Ruby's genetic makeup. As far as she was concerned, he didn't exist.

It was the only way she could look at her beautiful daughter and not fall apart.

Pen and paper and phone book in hand, Rachel sat down at the kitchen table as soon as she hung up from Debbie to start another list—this one for their nursery shopping expedition that evening. She wanted to be efficient, to know exactly what she wanted and where to go so she didn't wear Max out. He detested shopping and was being so sweet to offer to take her.

She'd call Ashley later, when her outer shell was a little less fragile. Her friend had a way of bulldozing information right out of Rachel. And something like this would bring out the worst in Ashley's tenaciousness.

Right now, more than anything, Rachel needed a little mental peace.

Shying away from any dangerous thoughts, she focused on the job at hand. When she finished the evening shopping list, she'd go back to the grocery one. She wanted to have that shopping done before Max got home. Starting tomorrow morning, the man was going to have meals in his own home.

He had her now.

She was somehow going to make that worthwhile.

One phone call to a children's furniture shop in San Antonio, no definitive answers, and a little voice came filtering down the stairs. Dropping her pen, Rachel raced up to the loft and straight in the door on the right-hand side. Ruby's room.

And Rachel's.

Her daughter was standing up in her portable crib. She pointed at Rachel as she walked in the door.

"Schee?" Ruby asked.

"I'm Mommy," Rachel said. She picked up the baby and set her on the bed for a change. Rachel was still a little clumsy with that part of her duties, but Ruby was old enough to know the drill and help Rachel out a bit. She lay placidly, lifting her legs when necessary, and stared at Rachel the entire time.

"Did you have a good sleep, punkin?" Rachel asked as she went about her work.

Ruby's little brow puckered, as though she were trying to decide. Or maybe she was trying to figure out who was wiping her bottom. Rachel couldn't be sure which it was.

"Mommy missed you," Rachel said, smiling at the little girl. Ruby's red hair was sticking to her head in sweaty ringlets, her green eyes so alert and knowing.

"I'm mommy," Rachel said, sliding a fresh disposable diaper underneath the baby. "Can you say mommy?"

Ruby grabbed for the baby wipe container beside them on the bed.

"Ma-ma," Rachel said more slowly. "Can you say ma-ma, Ruby?"

The corner of the container went straight into Ruby's mouth.

"Uck." Rachel took it away from the baby. "You don't want that."

Ruby bellowed. Not a slow buildup to a cry, which was all Rachel had heard to that point, but a full wail, complete with a red, screwed-up face and lung action that should never have been able to come out of one so little.

"What's wrong?" Rachel asked, checking quickly to see if she'd snapped the baby's skin into her overalls.

She couldn't have stuck her with a pin. There weren't any.

She checked the diaper anyway. Nothing.

And still the baby yelled. She was really mad about something.

Grabbing a wipe from the container, Rachel smoothed it over the baby's face, hoping the soothing feel would help calm her.

It didn't. But the container, which she'd set down within reach once again, did. Ruby picked it up, stopped crying immediately without so much as a hiccup, and promptly put the corner of the container back into her mouth.

"Aha!" Rachel grinned. "So you have a temper, little one." Tweaking the baby's nose lightly with her finger, she gently took the container away. "Sorry, punkin, but that's not good for you."

She scooped the baby up quickly, grabbed a plastic book from the top of the diaper bag Max had left on the dresser, and tried to distract Ruby with that. After a brief moment of rebellion, it worked. Rachel headed back downstairs with Ruby on her hip happily chewing on the book.

One disaster averted. She just might get the hang of this motherhood stuff sooner than she'd thought.

RUBY NEEDED to be fed. Pulling a jar of fruit out of the supply she had left from the day before, and a baby biscuit from the box Mrs. Butler had given her, Rachel set the baby up on a pillow on one of the big wooden chairs at Max's table, strapping her in with one of Max's belts.

"Here's your spoon," she said, handing the baby utensil Mrs. Butler had given her to the little girl. "Mrs. Butler says you like to use this."

With only a couple of tries, Ruby thrust the spoon into the bowl of mostly liquefied fruit and managed to get some of the globby mixture into her mouth.

"Okay," Rachel said, releasing her breath. "You're pretty good at that!"

Grabbing up her pen, she sat down opposite the baby and set to work. She had a lot of progress to make if she was going to be ready for Max in a few short hours. The evening shopping list—she quickly added a high chair to the growing column—and a grocery list. The trip into Trueblood to buy what was on the grocery list...

A large splat obstructed Rachel's view of the word she was writing.

Mixed fruit.

She glanced up. Ruby was wearing fruit on both cheeks, the underside of her nose, in one eyebrow, and across the side of her head. All in the space of time it had taken Rachel to make two entries on her list.

"Mrs. Butler forgot to mention that you've yet to master the art of using your spoon," she told the baby with a grin.

"Schee?" Ruby asked, holding both hands, including the one with a spoon full of fruit, up in the air.

You had to love a kid who could wear sticky fruit all over her body with complete unselfconsciousness.

"Yeah, I see," she said.

They were going to have to work on Ruby's vocabulary.

Right after they got the feeding thing handled.

Dropping her pen, Rachel retrieved a washcloth from the kitchen, cleaned up the baby, and sat down to feed her herself. At the rate Ruby had been going, she was never going to get full.

"I'll make a deal with you," she said, placing the biscuit in the baby's hand when she removed the spoon. "You do the dry hard stuff, and I do the wet mushy stuff. How's that?"

Mouth full, cheeks puffed out, Ruby stared wide-eyed at her new mother.

Rachel took that to mean yes.

As she scraped the last of the fruit from the bowl, her eye fell on her unfinished lists. Mentally adjusting her plans for the day, she rinsed the bowl while Ruby finished her biscuit. The groceries she could just wing. They needed everything.

As for the shopping that evening, she'd just have to do her best. It wasn't like Rachel not to be completely organized, with a well-thought-out plan.

But Ruby needed her.

And it felt damn good to be needed.

"MAX! I heard you were back." Dylan came around the side of his desk as Max arrived in the doorway of the Finders Keepers office upstairs at the ranch house.

"We got in late last night." He really wasn't looking forward to this meeting, feeling himself oddly defensive as he anticipated the questions Dylan was bound to have. Questions Max didn't want to answer, partly because he wasn't certain what those answers were.

Max sure as hell wasn't perfect. Not even close. But he always had the answers.

Leaning back against his desk, Dylan crossed his arms. "Lily said there was a baby with you."

Max started to ask how Lily knew that, but Dylan forestalled him. "She saw you guys driving into town this morning."

Leaving his hat on, hoping to make this a very short stay, Max nodded. "We went in to see Reverend Blair."

"And?"

"We're getting married next Saturday."

With a piercing look, Dylan dropped his arms. "No kidding," he said, no inflection in his voice. "Everything's been resolved then?"

"We're getting married," Max said, standing, feet apart, just inside the room. "I'm going to try to catch up on things here so that I can take a couple of days that next week after the wedding.''

"Whatever," Dylan said. "It's been so many years since you've had a real vacation you could take a month off and Dad wouldn't grumble." Dylan grinned. "Not much anyway. He'd just miss you like hell."

Max relaxed just a bit. He did a good job for the Garretts, worked long hours—as many as it took—to make the Double G the best it could be. He took pride in his work and loved his job.

He knew, too, that the Garretts appreciated all that he did.

But it still felt good to hear Dylan say so.

"I'm gone for a year," Dylan continued good-naturedly, "Dad thinks it was a month. You're gone for a day, he carries on like it was a year."

"Can I help it if your ugly mug is so forgettable?" Max asked, leaning nonchalantly in the doorway.

"Right." Dylan nodded, but his eyes promised retribution. "So tell me about the baby. I'm assuming it's the one I told you about. The Emersons' little girl?"

Max straightened. "You might as well know now. The baby is Rachel's. She had Ruby eighteen months ago in Austin, but gave her up for adoption."

Dylan's arms dropped. "To the Emersons," he guessed correctly.

Max nodded. "We're now in the process of adopting her."

Dylan's brow rose. "Which is why the wedding is back on so quickly."

"Rachel's staying at my place." Max wasn't going to be questioned. Not until he had some answers. And probably not even then. "We thought it was best for

Ruby to settle into a permanent home after being up-rooted so much in such a short time.''

"Just like that, you're a daddy?" Dylan asked.

It appeared that way. But Max couldn't find his way to being upset about that. As a matter of fact, he'd kind of hated to leave while Ruby was still asleep. He'd have liked to tell the runt goodbye.

"What are you doing, man?" Dylan asked, his gaze piercing.

"Taking care of the woman I'm going to marry."

Dylan tried—and failed—to bite back a frustrated scoff. "You've spent your entire life taking care of things, Max. First it was the small animals. From what I've heard, you were barely able to walk when your dad had you out helping him with chores."

"They needed to be done."

"By a toddler?"

"With my mother gone, he wanted to keep me with him."

"And while the rest of us guys were playing sports in school, you were here breaking horses."

"I enjoyed it," Max said. He couldn't see what Dylan was getting so hot about. "Sure beat the hell out of you during the rodeo days," he added. Rodeo was a sport.

"You competed once."

"And won."

"You took care of your dad after the accident," Dylan continued. "Nursed him until he died."

The rearing stallion had caught his father in the temple. Max's dad hadn't ever fully recovered his mental capabilities. That had been rough.

"What else was I going to do with him?" he said

now. "If it were William who'd been hurt, you and Lily and Ashley would have done the same."

"You were barely twenty when you took over here," Dylan said.

His friend was being stubborn as the mules they refused to have on their ranch and Max wasn't in the mood for it.

"It's my job," he said, chin jutting out. "A man has to make a living."

"I'm not denying that," Dylan said, standing, coming closer to Max. "I just want to know what's in it for you, Max? You spend your whole life taking care of other people. Who ever takes care of you?"

"I do." Thank you very much. What did Dylan think he was, for God's sake? "I don't need anybody looking after me."

"Everyone has needs."

Yeah. Max had a need. A big one. And in another week, when Rachel married him, if not before, he was going to get that woman in his bed and take care of that need in a big way.

"I'm not talking about sex." Dylan grinned.

Max was a little chagrined at the apparent ease with which Dylan had read his mind. But hey, Dylan was a man. And the closest thing to a brother Max had ever had. If a guy couldn't grouse about how horny he was with his brother, who else could he grouse with?

"Yeah, well, it's generally at the top of my list."

Settling one hip on the edge of an armchair, Dylan rested his forearm on his thigh. "I'm not sure you even have a list," he said.

Max took a step backward. "Conversation's a bit heavy for this early in the day," he said, and then, to spare Dylan's feelings, added, "at least without a shot or two to wash it down."

"I'm serious, Max," Dylan said. "I know you don't want to hear it, which is why I've never said anything before, but now, I don't know.... With all this stuff with Julie going on, and Lily and Ashley getting married, and Dad still alone, and then to have Rachel run out on you, it's just made me realize how short life is. And how precious love is."

"I love Rachel."

"I know." Dylan sighed. "But love isn't just about giving. It's about taking, too."

Pulling his hat down a little farther on his forehead in spite of the sweat ring that was urging him to take it off, Max said, "You're a smart one to talk, Dylan. Look at you and Julie. You've been giving to her for years. Anytime she called, you were there, willing to do whatever was needed. She married your best friend for God's sake, and you practically planned their whole wedding for them. And now, all these months of chasing her down—and now chasing Sebastian down—tell me, what have you gotten from her? What has she done for you?"

Dylan studied him with narrowed eyes.

"And what about the rest of your life? You're always there, ready to help whoever needs it. Pulling Ashley out of scraps. Standing in for Lily. Look at this business." Max gestured to the offices around him. "You spend your life finding lost people...."

"Okay." Dylan gave a wry chuckle and held up his hand. "Point taken."

Max relaxed a bit. Damn right it was. And about time, too. He wanted to be about the business of ranching, not engaged in an uncomfortable conversation with the ranch's heir.

"Sort of," Dylan added, standing. He moved back over behind his desk. "The difference between you and me, Max, is that I let other people do things for me, too. You don't."

The words hit Max harder than they should have. He was tired. It had been a crazy couple of days, filled with events he hadn't planned on.

Because he didn't have his usual ready comeback, he turned around and left.

CHAPTER THIRTEEN

RACHEL COULDN'T BELIEVE how much she missed Max
that afternoon. She'd been watching the clock for almost an hour before she finally heard his truck outside
in the yard.

It wasn't that she'd had a lot of time to sit around
and think about him. Ruby kept her running the entire
afternoon. It was just a sense of something vital missing—something she'd taken for granted over the last
couple of days.

"How was your afternoon?" he asked as soon as he
came through the door. His gaze took in the baby playing with a pan and a spoon in the middle of the living
room floor, and then Rachel, her long hair falling out
of the ponytail she'd—in desperation—pulled it into.

"Great!" she answered honestly. "I think Ruby
found absolutely everything on this floor that's a no-
no."

He chuckled, throwing his hat on the corner of a
chair. "That bad, huh?"

Actually, she'd had a blast. "The way I see it, we
got it all out of the way today, so tomorrow all that's
waiting are the yes-yeses."

He looked so great standing there, his jeans a little
dusty, his black hair wet with sweat. His grin made her
warm all over.

"I'd planned on having the grocery shopping done

by now," she told him, following him into the kitchen while he downed a tall glass of ice water. "Would you mind if we stop on our way home tonight so I can pick up the few things we'll need for breakfast? I can do the rest tomorrow after you leave for work."

She had mixed emotions about going into Trueblood the first time with Ruby. She dreaded it, actually, yet wanted to get it out of the way at the same time. And maybe, a small part of her was looking forward to showing off her beautiful daughter. How could anyone look at Ruby and see anything but goodness and light?

"Sure, we can stop," Max said. "You need more of that mush for the kid?" he asked.

"No." Rachel shook her head, arms crossed as she stood between the kitchen and the living room, watching both members of her new family. "We've got almost a full box."

"Then why stop?" Max asked, shaking his head. "You don't eat breakfast. Just coffee, and I know we've got plenty of that."

"For you," she said, staring at him. "I'm going to make you breakfast every morning. And dinner every night."

A man deserved meals in his own home.

"You don't have to do that. Especially not right now, while you're still settling in. I'm perfectly happy eating up with the guys."

"I don't mind," Rachel told him, trying not to be disappointed.

"Really." He ran one finger along her cheek, stopping at her bottom lip. "You don't need to bother yourself. I'll probably be up and gone before you wake up anyway."

Distracted as she was by the finger rubbing lightly

along her lip, Rachel nodded. He was probably right. She knew he had to be up and out at dawn. And there had always been more than enough good chow up at the ranch. Seemed kind of silly for her to drag herself out of bed to do something that didn't need doing.

But dang.

LATE THAT NIGHT, long after Ruby was sleeping soundly in her crib—the portable one until the new one was delivered—Rachel was awake in her room. She'd written in her journal. Read a couple of chapters of a book of which she couldn't remember the story. She'd unpacked as many of Ruby's new things as she had space for. Most of the larger furnishings were going to be delivered the next day.

She'd lain in bed and tried to count sheep. She'd allowed herself to think. And then forbidden herself to think. She'd even taken a couple of aspirin for the headache she felt coming.

And still, there she was, wide-awake.

So much had happened in so little time. And she was unsure about all of it.

Hoping to sneak past Max's door unnoticed—her almost husband was a light sleeper—Rachel headed stealthily for the stairs down to the main floor of the cabin. She'd left a couple of magazines down there. Maybe the easy reading would relax her.

She never got the chance to find out. She was almost in the living room when she noticed Max lounging in a big brown leather armchair, his feet propped up on a matching ottoman. He had a mostly empty glass of whiskey in his hand.

She turned as quickly and silently as she could to head back upstairs. He didn't look like he wanted to be interrupted. And she wasn't in the mood for conversation, either. Especially not late at night. And not with the man who was largely responsible for her insomnia.

"Don't go away without whatever you were coming down after on my account." The words weren't slurred, but he sounded exhausted.

Rachel stood still for a second, and then turned around. There was no point in pretending she hadn't come down.

"I was just going to get a magazine," she said lightly, moving quickly to retrieve the three on the coffee table that were all Ruby had left her.

She was so self-conscious, standing there in her black cotton boxers and T-shirt, while he was still wearing the jeans and shirt he'd changed into to go into town that evening.

He'd unbuttoned the shirt, though. Max had about the most beautiful chest she'd ever seen. And living in cowboy country, she'd seen a lot of chests.

"You'll have to find a place to stash those a little higher up," he said, noticing the slightly torn covers of the magazines she'd salvaged.

He didn't just sound tired; he looked it, too.

So why wasn't he up in bed? He had to be up at dawn.

"Something bothering you?" she asked softly, tentatively. Max spent so much time solving problems, he never seemed to have any.

"I'm fine," he said, taking a swig of his whiskey.

He hadn't really answered the question.

Rachel sat down on the edge of the couch, the magazines on her lap. She didn't have any idea what to say, only knew that this was a side to Max she'd never seen before. Knew, too, that she couldn't just go back upstairs and leave him like this.

"Everything okay down at the ranch?" she asked, searching for what might be on his mind.

"Fine. A few glitches, but nothing that wasn't easy enough to solve."

"And this ranch, it's okay, too?"

"Just fine. There's been enough water, the fields are lush and full, about as good for grazing as a man can ask."

She nodded, biting her lower lip slowly. "You having second thoughts about having me and Ruby here?"

"God, no!" He took another long swig of whiskey—his Adam's apple bobbing as he swallowed—and then set the glass down on the table beside him.

Rachel took a second to absorb the relief the vehemence of that reply brought her. And then she just sat.

In some ways, she didn't know Max at all. She knew he was honest, completely reliable, hardworking, quiet, gentle, kind, gorgeous, sexy as hell, funny in a quiet sort of way, well-liked and respected by everyone who knew him. She knew what he was thinking sometimes, knew that he loved movies and hated to shop, that he was good at every sport he tried, and that he mostly found them a waste of time. She knew that he loved her. And still, sitting there, she was with a stranger.

"What was it like growing up here?" she asked him. She didn't know why she'd never thought to ask before. She'd known him her whole life. His being at the Double G had always just been a given.

She'd never thought about his life from his perspective.

"The best," he said, laying his head back against the leather headrest. "All I've ever wanted to do was ranch, and it doesn't get any better than the Double G.'' His hands were folded across his stomach. The knots in Rachel's own stomach dissipated just a bit. He seemed more relaxed than he had when she'd first come down.

"Yeah, but what about before you were old enough to ranch, when you were too young to know that's what you wanted to do?"

He shrugged. "I was born knowing."

Thinking of him as a baby made her smile. She imagined him Ruby's size, having his diaper changed. He'd probably changed it himself. Or maybe he'd just come out potty trained. Grinning to herself, she wondered what it had been like for his mother, having a baby like Max. Had he always been so self-sufficient?

"How old were you when your mother died?" she asked. She knew he'd been young, preschool, but she'd figured his mother had been there through his toddler years.

"Six months."

"So you don't even remember her."

He shook his head.

"Who took care of you after that?" She'd never heard him, or anyone, mention a nanny.

"My father."

"I mean while he was ranching." The senior Mr. Santana had been foreman of the Double G his entire life.

"Even then."

"How could he be out on the range and taking care of you at the same time?"

Max looked over at her and grinned. "Taught me how to carry my own weight."

Staring at him, Rachel didn't know what to say. She didn't think that was funny at all.

"And how does a six-month-old baby 'carry his own weight?'" she asked. Ruby was having a hard time figuring out how to get a spoon of food from her bowl to her mouth and she was a full year older than Max had been when his mother died.

"Well, maybe not quite then," Max said. "From what I've been told, he made a sturdy carrier for his back and carried me around like a papoose. I cut my teeth mostly on the leather of his horse's bridle."

"That's horrible!" Rachel cried.

"No, it's not," Max countered. "My father taught me all the most important lessons. How to work hard, be kind, love what I do, always be honest, and to take care of myself. They've served me well."

Thinking of all the toys they'd purchased that evening, many at Max's insistence every time Ruby showed any interest in something, she asked, "When did you ever have time to play?"

"At night, after the work was done. My dad loved cards." He smiled. "Some of my best memories are nights down at the Double G bunkhouse playing cards with the guys."

"When you were older, maybe," she said, leaning forward, her hands on her chin. "But what about when you were still a little boy?" A toddler like Ruby, beating on pans, wearing puréed fruit, and tearing up magazines.

"Even then," Max said. He crossed one ankle over the other. "I was about two the first time I held a hand of cards. But ten before I actually won a round."

"What about your schoolwork?"

He shrugged. "I got it done."

"So the guys helped you with that before you all started to play cards?"

"Nah. I just did it."

He just did it. Like he just did everything else in his life.

Rachel found the whole thing rather depressing.

"You'd best get that beautiful butt upstairs before I try to convince you to share it with me," Max drawled, pulling Rachel out of her reverie.

Her heart started to pound. She felt suddenly naked, sitting there in nothing but little pieces of cotton, her long legs bare for him to stare at.

As he was doing.

That look almost tempted her to stay.

"Okay." She jumped up. "I guess I'm more tired than I thought."

"Me, too," Max said. His feet fell to the floor and he stood, taking his glass with him. Rachel waited while he put the glass in the dishwasher and turned off the kitchen light. She turned out the living room one herself, and as they headed up the stairs together, she was intensely aware of him right behind.

How much of her behind could he see underneath the extrawide legs of her too short boxers?

She hoped it was a lot.

And that he liked what he saw.

Passing his door, Rachel wondered, fleetingly, what would happen if she went through that door. Her breath quickened, liquid fire pooling in her belly. And then she felt his heat behind her and moved on to her own room.

He followed her, pulling her to a stop just outside her door.

"You're very beautiful, you know that?" he whispered, pushing a lock of hair away from the side of her face.

Turning her face into the gentle caress, Rachel nodded. She needed this man. Needed him so desperately.

He came closer, pushing her body against the wall with the slow pressure of his hips against hers.

Rachel forced herself not to push against him. To accept the loving embrace he was offering. An embrace she wanted arguably more than he did.

She wasn't surprised when his lips found hers. Was even able to lose herself in the delicious fire of that kiss for a moment. Until his body hardened insistently and she knew that in another second there would be no going back.

Max pulled away before she could.

"I've waited this long to do this your father's way, I'm not going to buckle now," he said with a self-deprecating grin. "I want to be able to look my father-in-law in the eye when I sit across from him at our wedding dinner."

"It's a little late for that, Max," she reminded him. She just couldn't do the protected virgin stuff anymore.

She wasn't a virgin.

She'd been there. Done it all. And then had a baby.

"It's never too late, Rach," he said softly. "One mistake doesn't mean that ten more are okay. And conversely, doing it right now doesn't lose value because of a mistake in the past."

Rachel was tired enough to find the logic in that. And be comforted.

With a grateful smile, she stood up on tiptoe, gave Max one last, full kiss, and slipped inside her door, shutting it behind her before he could see the tears that had sprung to her eyes.

If she wasn't careful, the man was going to make her feel like the good girl she'd been raised to be. The girl she'd always thought herself—until the night that changed her life forever.

Maybe doing things right this time would have a value of its own, maybe even restore some of her sense of self-worth. Looking over at Ruby, she sure hoped so. Because one thing she knew for certain.

There was no going back.

Not to that night more than two years ago in Austin, the night everything had gone so horribly wrong.

And not to last week, when she was a giddy bride, seemingly without a care in the world.

For better or worse, she was a mother.

And, in one short week, she was going to have to be a wife.

RACHEL GOT UP the next morning to see Max off, after all. She was awake anyway. And already missed him. She wanted to tell him goodbye. To see him before he went off for his day.

He'd made a pot of coffee and she poured one for herself while she waited for him to come down from his shower.

Because she was going to wait until after he left to take her own shower, she'd just pulled on her bathrobe over her pajamas and brushed her teeth in the half bath downstairs. So far she and Max had managed to co-exist with only one full bathroom without running into each other. She hadn't moved her toiletries in yet—just kept carrying her little suitcase with her when she showered.

She was a little nervous about impinging on his space. Max had been living alone a long time.

Perhaps she was a bit self-conscious, too. And she hated that. She loved Max so much. When would the past stop preventing her from relaxing and just going with that love?

"You didn't have to get up."

She looked up to see him almost at the bottom of the stairs. He'd come down without his boots on—probably to be quiet and not wake her and Ruby.

She shrugged. "I was awake. And I wanted to tell you goodbye."

He grinned, as though her answer had pleased him. "You smelled the coffee and wanted a cup," he teased.

"That, too."

He'd carried his cup down with him and refilled it, taking a sip while still standing at the counter. "What are you planning to do today?"

"Grocery shopping first," she said. She'd actually made a mental list for the entire day in the long hours she'd lain awake during the night. "Then back here for Ruby's morning nap and lunch and to meet the furniture guys. I'm hoping to get a lot of work done on the nursery this afternoon, get stuff unpacked and put away."

"Wait for me if there's any heavy work to be done," he said, leaning back against the counter. For someone who, according to him, usually had his hat on his head five minutes after he got out of bed, he didn't seem to be in any hurry to leave.

"I'm hoping I can just get them to put things where I want them to go. We already know they're going to be setting up the crib." They'd made those arrangements at the store the night before.

He nodded. "You'll really be able to settle her in after next week when we get the spare bed out of there."

She didn't want to think about that right now. Had spent far too much time trying not to think about it— or trying to find a way to handle thinking about it— during the night.

"I'm also planning to get some laundry done," she said. They'd been away since Saturday; he'd have several days' worth of clothes she could wash for him. And because she'd yet to move her clothes over from her room at the rectory, she was down to one clean outfit.

"I already did a lot of it," he told her, rinsing his empty cup in the sink. "I threw a load of jeans in last night while you were upstairs putting things away, and then did another load when I came down to make the coffee this morning."

Oh.

"I guess I'll just do mine and Ruby's then."

"I threw whatever you had in the hamper upstairs in with my stuff."

Oh.

"Thanks," she said, hoping she sounded more properly grateful than she felt. Was there nothing the man wasn't perfectly happy to do for himself?

"I left Ruby's stuff, though," he added, grabbing his hat and putting it on his head before he slipped into the cowboy boots he'd brought down with him. "I wasn't sure if you washed it in a regular-size washer."

She smiled, telling herself not to feel superfluous. He was only trying to help. And she loved him for that.

"I don't think they make baby-size washers," she said.

Max shrugged and she thought he looked just a tad self-conscious. The look was rather cute on him. "I didn't know if maybe her stuff got washed by hand."

"Nope," Rachel said. "If it's durable enough to survive Ruby, it can survive the washing machine. I'll do it this afternoon."

At least she had Ruby to take care of.

Max dropped a quick kiss on her lips and then stopped just short of the door to turn around again. "You sure you want to go into town this morning?" he asked, looking concerned.

"Of course."

"I just—" He hesitated, took his hat off, put it back on again. "I thought maybe we'd go in together. We could go tonight when I get home."

"Then I can't make dinner—I know, I know," she said with barely a pause. "You don't need me to make dinner. But while you're perfectly happy to eat chow with the boys, I'm not. I need dinner."

"We could pick something up at Boots. Food's good there."

The place did have a few tables, but the crowd it drew went there for the long antique bar and selection of beers. "I don't think it's a great place to take Ruby."

"So we'll eat at Camelita's." Trueblood's only diner.

He couldn't possibly prefer to go into town and eat out with a baby and grocery shop after a long day on the ranch. But she knew better than to say that.

Rachel shook her head. "It's okay, Max. I'd rather go this morning. That way I can take my time with the shopping. And I've eaten out so much over the past week, I'm going through withdrawal for a home-cooked meal.''

He still didn't look convinced.

''I'll be okay,'' she told him softly, moved by what she knew was really concerning him. ''I'm a big girl, Max, I can handle any fallout that comes my way.''

''I know you can,'' he said. And she could tell he meant it. ''I'd just like to be there with you.''

Rachel stood, her arms wrapped around her middle. ''I think this is something I need to do on my own.''

After a long silent look, Max nodded. He pulled her close for a lingering kiss and then let her go.

''If anyone bites, bite back,'' he said, and then was gone.

Rachel was still grinning when she heard Ruby fuss to get up a few minutes later.

The man definitely had a way with words.

CHAPTER FOURTEEN

MAX WAS A BIT surprised to see William Garrett riding out to where he was working on a fence line. Max could have sent one of the boys to do the job, but after a morning of overseeing everyone else, he'd needed to get out on the land and do some work himself.

Truth be known, he'd been eager for some time to himself. Things were going on inside him, in his mind and his emotions, that he wasn't completely comfortable with.

"Something wrong?" he asked the older man, when he pulled up and dismounted.

"Nothing."

Max hadn't thought so. William hadn't been riding fast enough for an emergency. But still, his sudden appearance was odd.

"Things are looking good," Max said, returning to the job at hand. "The fields are going to see us through the hot summer months without a problem. Looks like we've got a bigger herd than we'd hoped, as well."

William nodded, his leathery face inexpressive and his usually lively blue eyes somber.

Stopping what he was doing, Max removed his hat, wiped the sweat from his brow and then returned his hat to his head. He pulled it a little lower this time. The fence was almost done. He wished William would state his case and get on with it.

"I imagine Dylan's talked to you." Max finally forced the issue when it appeared that William was going to be content to stand there and watch him for the rest of the afternoon.

"You didn't come in for lunch," William said, deftly sidestepping the question.

"I grabbed a sandwich before I came out," Max said. "I've been gone, didn't want to waste any time."

"You should have been there," William said. "With you gone, the boys were free to talk their damn fool heads off."

Max tensed. "And...?"

"Seems you've been like a bitch in the middle of a breech birth all morning."

Max grunted. "There's a lot to do, getting caught up from the days I was gone," he said. There wasn't much truth in that statement, though. There'd been no catastrophes the few days he'd been away. His men were great for the everyday stuff. They knew what to do and did it. "Looks like I'm going to be gone again in another week," he added. "Wasn't time for bull-shitting around for an hour before any work got done."

"Maybe." William frowned, squinting beneath the brim of his hat. The sun was bright that morning, but even the sun couldn't reach beneath the brim of William's impressive hat. "That any reason to grouch at Mike for putting your saddle on the wrong hook?"

Mike was a new kid helping them out part-time in the tack barn.

"Everything's clearly marked. It was a foolish mistake. Cost me time I didn't have to lose."

William moved forward, leaning against the part of the fence that was fully repaired.

"You're the best foreman this ranch has ever had," William said. "And that includes your father."

Max grunted, pleased with the compliment, and grabbed his saddlebag from the ground at his feet. Pulling out the pliers, he adjusted some wire on the fence. He didn't look at William.

"You're also one of the kindest men I've ever met. This morning wasn't like you."

"I griped at a boy," Max said, trying to rein in his irritation. "Sue me."

"You barked out orders like this was the damned army, told another guy that your business was your own when he inquired about how you were doing—"

"Okay, okay," Max interrupted, holding up one hand. "I'm a little short on sleep."

"You've gone nights without sleeping more times than I can count. What with birthing foals, bad weather, lost cows. More than one night at a time, too."

Slinging his saddlebag over the fence, Max turned and faced William, meeting the other man's gaze head-on.

"I've got a lot on my mind. I'll be more aware with the boys. I'm sorry." What in hell was the matter with him, letting it show? Max never let anything show. Never had. Not when he'd had to walk the range with blisters the size of golf balls on his feet because his father had forgotten to buy him new boots between his eighth and ninth birthday. Not when his dad had had his accident. Not when Rachel had run out on him.

"I'm not looking for an apology, son," William said, those damn eyes still far too subdued. "What I'm doing is wondering if you're doing the right thing. I'm just asking you to give it some thought before it's too late."

Max didn't need a father. He'd had one.

And his own dad had never interfered with Max's decisions. No one had.

"I'm doing the right thing." This wasn't up for discussion.

With a penetrating look, William studied Max silently for a moment. "You sound pretty sure about that," he finally said.

"I am." He was. The choice to marry Rachel, to adopt Ruby had been a no-brainer.

"Because it's what you want, or because it's what Rachel needs?"

"Both."

"You're sure about that?"

"Absolutely."

Was that it then? Could they get on with the business of being men and working the land that would beat them if they didn't stay on top of it every second of every day?

But William didn't seem to be in any hurry to get back to his office at the house, and the work he surely had waiting for him there.

"So what's eating you then, if it's not the wedding and ready-made family?"

Max pushed the toe of his boot against the soft dirt surrounding the post he'd just reinforced, a pat answer eluding him.

Which was discomfiting in itself.

William waited patiently. And before he knew what he was doing, Max heard himself ask, "Did you change when you married Elizabeth?"

Everyone knew how much William and his wife had adored each other, how happy they were together.

"Change how?" William asked, looking off in the direction from which he'd come.

His work on the fence finished, Max moved over to his horse and hooked the saddlebag back where it belonged. "No way," he grunted. "Forget I ever said anything."

"I might forget," William said, moving back to his own horse. "But I don't think you're going to."

Max was uncomfortably sure that William was right on that one.

Both men mounted up and started back in the direction of the ranch. "Sure I changed when I married Elizabeth." William rode up beside Max once they'd set an even pace. "I wanted to be home more, for one thing."

Max ticked that one off his list. It wasn't really what had been bothering him, but it was still good to know that William—a man he respected greatly—had been there, too.

"I was more preoccupied," William continued. "Suddenly had other things to think about. Things that had never mattered before started to matter."

Max wanted to ask what kind of things, but couldn't.

"I didn't used to much care about danger, or even think about taking chances, but once I had Elizabeth at home, and the little ones, I got a bit more cautious."

Made sense.

Max didn't have a problem with that.

"I looked forward to the end of the day," William said with a faraway grin on his face. "Thought about sex a lot."

Yeah, he'd been there for months. He *knew* that was normal.

"That's about it," William said a moment later, riding next to Max in silence.

Damn.

Max wasn't completely sure what in the hell was eating at him, but he knew it wasn't anything William had mentioned.

He just felt unsettled somehow, like he was losing control of something.

It made no sense at all. He was gaining a wife, a family, more responsibility. Not losing control.

Shaking his head, he kicked his horse up to a gallop, vowing to put the whole thing out of his mind once and for all. He loved Rachel to distraction.

Couldn't wait to marry her. Honest to God couldn't wait.

That's what he'd spend the next seven days thinking about.

And the rest, like any bad behavior, would go away if ignored.

IT WAS AFTERNOON before Rachel made it into town. The deliverymen showed up early, Ruby got cereal in her hair and needed a bath, and then it was time for her nap, and for lunch, from which another mess resulted. And another bath.

Number one on Rachel's grocery list was food that the baby could feed herself without needing three baths, and outfits, a day. Ruby was eager to be independent and Rachel didn't want to discourage her.

Her stomach churned as she drove the ten miles into Trueblood's grocery cum gas station cum feed store cum post office. With the place offering so many services for the town, it was also where most of the locals could be found.

And Rachel knew every one of them. Many of the older folks had known her since she was born—they had offered the support that had seen her through her mother's death during her senior year in high school. They'd all, at one time or another, encouraged her—the preacher's kid who was such a nice girl, always helping out, never giving her father a lick of trouble, setting an example for the rest of the kids.

The list went on and on. Rachel was certain it didn't include giving birth to a baby outside of marriage.

It was Friday. Payday. Trueblood's grocery and feed store was doing a booming business. With Ruby on her hip, Rachel breezed into the fray, got herself a shopping cart, threaded her daughter's chubby little legs between the bars of the seat in the front of it, strapped her in, and—

"Rachel?" Ellie, one of her father's older parishioners and the wife of a rancher with a small spread just five miles from town, had just come out of the store pushing a cart full of shopping bags. "I didn't know you were back."

Rachel smiled and nodded, hoping that her nervousness wasn't showing. "Got back the day before yesterday," she said.

Ellie was speaking to Rachel, but couldn't seem to pull her eyes away from the baby in the cart. And neither could everyone else passing by. Her seventh-grade English teacher, the organist from church, a woman who'd been two years ahead of her in school who was carrying a baby about Ruby's age. Pretty soon there was an entire crowd around Rachel. She couldn't have pushed her way into the store if she'd wanted to.

For a split second, she wished Max were there. He'd create a tunnel for her to pass through.

Except that she'd meant it when she'd told him that morning that she needed to do this on her own.

"Everyone," she said, including them all in her smile, "this is my daughter, Ruby." And before they could do more than gasp, she continued lightly, "Max and I are adopting her. We're getting married next Saturday and you're all invited. Everything's going exactly as planned, just a couple of weeks later. Oh..." She stopped and took her daughter's little hand in her own. "Except that we have a flower girl now."

"Did you say your daughter?"

"Does your father know?"

"Is Max her father?"

"Where's she been?" were four of the questions Rachel was able to make out. You'd think she was a president-elect facing the press after the announcement of his election win.

Except that in the crowd surrounding her—a crowd that appeared to be growing—there were some silent members.

Those were the ones that made Rachel the most nervous.

"I—"

"Hey." Debbie Anderson pushed her way through the gathering crowd to Rachel's side. "So this is little Ruby," she said, as though she'd known long before the day before about the baby's existence. "Hi, sweetie!" She ran a hand through Ruby's bright red curls, tickled her neck. "Welcome to Trueblood."

Ruby studied Debbie with that discerning stare. Debbie laughed. Rachel would have joined in if she hadn't been surrounded by so many questions she couldn't answer.

"Come on, everybody," Debbie said, turning back

to the crowd. "Give the little one some breathing room or she won't like her hometown at all and she has a lot of years here ahead of her."

Slowly, people started to dissipate. A couple moved forward as the crowd thinned, as though they thought they knew Rachel well enough to get the explanation the others were going to have to do without.

"I was just going in to get some groceries," Debbie said. "Mind if I share your basket?"

Rachel shook her head, smiled at her father's parishioners, and went on her way.

There were going to be questions. Lots of them.

And nowhere near the answers to match them.

People would talk. Rumors would be passed around. Conclusions drawn. And then life was going to go on.

They could tsk-tsk all they wanted to, but they couldn't hurt Rachel. And since she'd taken herself out of her father's home, he should be safe from any damage as well.

"You've lived in this town a lot longer than I have," Debbie said as they picked over heads of lettuce. "Don't you ever get tired of the prying?"

"Schee?" Ruby said.

"You want to see?" Rachel asked, holding a head of lettuce for the baby to touch. "It's lettuce. You're too little to have any right now, but if you're anything like your mama, you're going to love lettuce."

With her lettuce in the cart, Debbie moved on to the cucumbers. Rachel followed.

"I don't get tired of Trueblood," she said, answering Debbie's earlier question. "The people here care about each other, about what's going on in each other's lives. I don't see that as prying."

"But they're so judgmental sometimes."

"Not really." Rachel shook her head and gave Ruby a cucumber to hold. "They have their opinions, but they're basically good people. Some are going to disapprove, but only until they get over their shock. I mean, who'd have thought the preacher's kid would come home after skipping out on her own wedding with a toddler in tow?"

"Rachel!"

Rachel turned as the woman who rented rooms at the motel came running up to her.

"I heard you were back," Maggie said.

Rachel had known Maggie her entire life and it always seemed that she had on the same outfit. Some kind of shapeless flowered shirt that had no beginning or ending and a pair of pastel polyester pants. Winter or summer. Church or sweeping the motel parking lot.

"Got back Wednesday night," Rachel said, unconsciously moving in front of Ruby.

"Heard about the wee one, too," Maggie said. Rachel almost grinned at how fast the news was traveling. They should be over this hurdle within days, not the weeks or months it could have taken.

Maggie peered around Rachel to look at Ruby. The baby stared back, clutching her cucumber to her chest.

"She's really yours, ain't she?" Maggie said, sounding amazed. "I mean, look at her. She looks just like you did when you were that age."

And this was why Rachel loved Trueblood so much—because in the grocery store, she could run into someone who knew her when she was born. Trueblood was home. Her people were family.

"She's really mine," Rachel said.

"Where's her daddy?" Maggie asked, still peering

at Ruby as though she'd have her parentage posted on her forehead. "Who's her daddy?"

Debbie had moved closer, but she didn't rescue Rachel this time.

"Max is her daddy now," Rachel said. And with both hands on her cart, she slowly pushed it away.

Debbie walked beside her silently. There was no way Rachel could give the other woman what she wanted. An explanation. The truth. Even if she got beyond the panic and found a safe enough place to travel back again and relive that experience without falling apart, she'd still shrivel up with shame.

She wasn't the main reason the truth must remain hidden forever. That reason was sitting in the basket in front of her.

She'd die before she ever exposed her precious little girl to the truth of her conception. She couldn't bear the thought of Ruby carrying that burden.

It was one of the reasons she'd opted for adoption in the first place. So Ruby would never know the true circumstances behind her birth....

A couple of seconds later, Maggie came running up behind them again. "Rachel, I know you're getting married next week and all, but since the wedding plans were already done, I was hoping you might have some time this week."

"Sure," Rachel said automatically. Since her mother died, whenever Rachel was home, she'd fallen quite naturally into helping out whenever her father's parishioners—who were most of the people in Trueblood, since his church was the only one there—needed something.

"Miz Abby's daughter, Beth, had her baby a couple of days ago."

"But that's almost six weeks early," Rachel said.

"Yeah, and the little one's going to be in the hospital in San Antonio for a while and her mama wants to be with her, but refuses to go because of the little ones at home."

"We can arrange for child care," Rachel said, her mind already running through the church roster for stay-at-home moms who would be willing to help out.

"We've already done that," Maggie said. "But Beth won't hear none of it. She says she can't put everyone out that way."

"I offered to keep them during the evenings," Debbie said. "Beth wouldn't hear of it."

"I'll talk to her," Rachel promised both women. "We'll work something out."

"I knew it," Maggie said, practically bouncing up and down in her rightness. "I told 'em soon as you got back you'd take care of it."

Rachel grinned, asked about the baby and Beth, and stood back while Maggie tickled Ruby's nose with the leafy ends of the carrots she was buying.

Ruby laughed, but not before she'd checked to make certain that Rachel was right there first.

After only a couple of days the baby was claiming ownership.

And this was what life was all about, Rachel thought. Being surrounded by friends and loved ones who needed her.

She couldn't wait to get home and tell Max all about it.

The thought pulled her up short. She couldn't tell Max.

He wouldn't understand.

And suddenly, standing there in the produce department of the feed and grocery story, Rachel realized what the problem was between her and Max. He was right. She didn't trust him.

Not with her heart.

Because while he might love her, he didn't need her.

Not to tell his troubles to, that was for sure. She wasn't sure if he even allowed himself to have any. He just had solutions.

Not to cook for him. Or do his laundry.

If she hadn't had Ruby to care for these past two days in Max's home, she'd have felt utterly useless being there.

Why hadn't she realized all this before? Was it because she'd been too busy running from herself to see beyond her own panic?

Rachel continued with her shopping, trying to follow and participate in Debbie's conversation—at least enough so that her friend didn't suspect that Rachel's world was falling apart all over again. Yet the entire time her mind was reeling as so many things fell into place.

And the more they fell, the more sadness engulfed her.

She'd been so busy seeing all of the signs that Max really loved her—something she'd been dreaming about for more than half her life—that she'd missed the fact, consciously at least, that he didn't need her.

Listening last night as Max had talked about his childhood, she'd known that something essential was wrong with the picture he'd drawn. The man had spent his entire life learning not to need anyone but himself. Always on the outside looking in. On his father's life. His father's card games. The Garrett family. And what had Max's place been?

To help. Himself and anyone and everyone else. Animal and human alike. It was all he knew. To be needed. Not to need.

Max didn't need her.

And until he did, she wasn't safe needing him, either.

So where did that leave either one of them?

CHAPTER FIFTEEN

THE DAYS TOOK ON a pattern of sorts. Rachel got up in the morning to see Max off to work. She had dinner waiting when he got home at night. Together they bathed Ruby, read to her, and put her to bed.

And then together spent the next couple of hours trying to pretend they weren't alone together in his cabin. Trying to pretend that everything was okay. That they were okay.

Max made it through the weekend—barely—and only then because Sunday was taken up with church, fending off curious looks, concerns, hesitant well-wishes and questions, and dinner at his soon-to-be father-in-law's house, prepared by his soon-to-be wife.

By Monday night, he was tense as a tiger on a two-week fast.

The wedding was only five days away and Rachel didn't seem to have progressed at all toward a desire to see it happen. If anything, she'd taken herself further away from Max. Perhaps it was just his imagination but it didn't seem as if she was letting him do anything to help her.

It was always done before he knew it needed doing.

Yet, as she sat quietly on the couch Monday after Ruby was in bed, reading a magazine rather than regaling him with anecdotes from her day—anecdotes he'd grown to enjoy over the preceding months of their relationship—Max knew that something wasn't right.

He just had no idea what it was.

"You still planning to get married on Saturday?"

He hadn't meant to blurt the words out like that, but he had to know. He couldn't stand another five days of waiting to see if she'd hang around this time.

She looked up, eyes wide. "Of course."

"You sound sure about that."

"I am." And then with a frown, she asked, "Aren't you?" He caught a glimpse of the need in her eyes and didn't fight the relief that followed.

"Yes," he told her, meeting her gaze head-on.

Rachel looked down. She'd left him again.

"What's happened to us, Rach?" he asked after several minutes of watching her, the silence in the remote cabin an indication of what he feared was to come.

"What do you mean?" She was frowning, her green eyes truly perplexed.

"We used to fill every minute we were together with conversation—either verbal or not. I could always tell what you were thinking. Or at least get close. Now we can't seem to find enough to say to each other to fill an hour after dinner."

She shrugged. "We've never lived together before."

"We aren't living together now."

She pulled at the collar of her turtleneck. "In all ways but one we are."

He didn't agree. "We're sharing a roof. And a baby."

She stared at him silently, as though struggling with something. Something she wanted to say? Or something she didn't.

"Let me in, babe," he said softly. "I'm not the enemy."

"I know that." Her voice was husky, barely above a whisper.

"We're acting like an old married couple and we aren't even a young married couple yet," he said, trying desperately to reach her.

In all the catastrophes he'd handled in his life, natural disasters included, he'd never been up against one as tough as this.

Or one that mattered as much.

"We're just adjusting, Max," she told him, her voice pleading with him to let it go. "We've been through a lot of changes in a very short period of time."

Was that all it was then? She just needed time? He'd love to think so.

But he didn't.

"I didn't think we'd ever reach this point," he said, being completely honest with her. "Even when we were an old married couple, I thought we'd be different."

"We are different," she said, her brows raised with the level of her sincerity.

Throwing down the cattle report he'd been pretending to read, Max moved over to join her on the couch, though even then, he didn't touch her.

Didn't trust her to welcome the advance—this woman he was due to make his wife in less than a week.

"If we're so different," he said, facing her, "why can't you talk to me anymore? Is it something I said? I've hurt you in some way?"

"No!" Reaching out, Rachel ran her slim, soft fingers lightly down Max's cheek. It was the first time she'd voluntarily touched him since that kiss had gotten so far out of hand outside her bedroom door the previous week.

Max absorbed the touch like a dehydrated field absorbed rain. Quickly. Greedily. As though the one drop might be the last.

"You've done far more than I deserve, Max. I love you so much for that. And I'm more grateful than you'll ever know."

"So what's the problem?"

She looked at him, her green eyes imploring, sorry, confused. Confusing him. "I just need time," she finally whispered.

Time.

It was something he had. Something he was willing to give if it could help her in some way.

But how could he be sure that was all she needed? Especially when his gut was telling him something very different.

Moving closer to her, Max slid an arm around her shoulders, telling himself that if he could just get close to her, physically, just sit there and enjoy her warmth, he'd be okay.

Sex was probably the problem. They both just needed it. They'd been living in too close quarters, wanting each other for too long for it not to be affecting them.

Before he knew what he was doing, before he could tell himself it wasn't a good idea, Max leaned down, pushed the long, silky red hair back from Rachel's neck and started nuzzling her there. Just little kisses, tiny tastes of the nectar he really wanted.

She felt like satin, smelled like fresh mountain air and roses, tasted so sweet and good he couldn't stop.

"Mmm." Rachel's groan was almost too much for him.

Without conscious thought, Max was lying with her on the couch, and was kissing her like he'd never kissed her before. Like a man who was claiming what was his.

His lips were hungry, devouring hers, tasting her mouth, her tongue. Making love to her with a plunge and retreat that left no doubt what lay ahead for the two of them.

And Rachel was kissing him right back, dueling with him, clinging to his body with as much need as was coursing through his own. He could feel her taut nipples through the fabric of their shirts. Was pleased in a very masculine way to find that she wasn't wearing a bra, that there was one less barrier between him and his goal.

He'd touched her breasts before, but never without clothes impeding him, reminding him. But he was beyond reminder. Beyond restraint and control. If making love to Rachel was the only way to get her back, to connect with her again, then he had no choice.

And even if his mind had one, he was pretty sure his body no longer did. This close to her, he couldn't even think about stopping. About denying himself—or her—the release that would set them both free.

"Mmm" she moaned again, differently. His passion-glazed brain couldn't translate that moan. He just knew that her busy tongue was driving him to distraction.

With a deftness born of too much experience, he had the buttons of her shirt undone in record time, and then, finally, gloriously, painfully, his palm splayed across her naked breast, touching for the first time that beautiful, soft, full splendor that was all woman.

Only woman.

Her womanhood was her weapon.

And she'd stabbed him so thoroughly Max was never going to recover. He was going to be in bondage to this woman for the rest of his life. And beyond. He knew that more surely than he knew anything else in life.

"You're so beautiful," he whispered against her lips, his thumb flicking across her hardened nipple.

The look on Rachel's face was odd. She was smiling with her mouth, but her eyes...

They weren't there with him. Didn't seem to be really seeing him at all.

"You okay, babe?" he whispered, pulling back enough to give her some space.

She blinked, focused on Max, and nodded. With a hand at the back of his neck, she pulled his mouth back down to hers.

And Max had no strength at all to deny her whatever she asked.

He kissed her lips. Her cheeks and chin and eyelids. The tip of her nose. Always coming back to gorge himself on her lips again.

And then he traveled lower, seeing her breasts in their completely naked glory for the first time as he bent to taste them. He'd meant to take things slow, to explore her with soft kisses first, then maybe with his tongue. Instead, he suckled her as if she were his very lifeblood.

"Mmm." Her moan was completely recognizable that time. He was pleasing her. "Oh, Max," she said with a husky voice. "More, please." She sounded surprised, desperate. Excited.

She sounded like she was discovering feelings she'd never felt before—which, considering that baby upstairs, didn't make sense at all.

Next time he'd take it slow. Explore all of her. Arouse every nerve ending in her body.

With one swift flick, he had the button on her jeans open and the zipper down. His hand slid beneath the elastic of her panties and...

"No!"

The cry sent chills clear through to Max's soul. And next thing he was sitting hard on his butt on the living room floor, his shoulder throbbing from an encounter with the coffee table.

"No," Rachel said again, much more softly. This time the word was accompanied by a spate of choking sobs. Horrible sounds. Wounded, diseased sounds.

He couldn't think. Couldn't understand. He felt completely lost.

"Rach?" he asked hesitantly, still sitting where she'd pushed him.

His whole body ached—his throbbing groin most of all.

But from the sound of her, the look of her, she was feeling a pain he couldn't even imagine.

And he had no idea why.

"I'M SORRY." Rachel forced the words out through the haze. Huddled on the couch, trembling, she was still caught up in the paralyzing darkness.

"What's going on, Rach?"

Max was only a cloud in the background, a familiar

voice that was disconcerting, increasing her agitation as it asked for things she couldn't give.

"Rach?"

He wasn't coming any closer. Relief allowed a small measure of coherence to infiltrate the dark storm enveloping her.

"I'm sorry," she said again. Breathe. They'd taught her how to breathe when these attacks came on. In through the nose. Out through the mouth. Breathe.

She concentrated on the counselor's soothing words. The breaths were short, forced, painful at first, but she kept working them. She knew what to do. Breathe. And as soon as she could see, focus on a color. Find one that she liked. Count how many times she saw it.

"What is it?" Max asked. He sounded concerned. "What's happening, Rachel? Let me help you."

Max. From the other world. The one she was trying so hard to fit into.

Air came a little easier and the trembling calmed enough for her to straighten her cramped legs, to relax her arms, which had a death grip around her chest. She still couldn't see much in her peripheral vision, but she knew that would come.

She knew the ropes, the stages of panic, what to expect from her traumatized psyche and reactive body. It had just been a long time since she'd been through a full-scale attack. Well over a year.

She'd hoped they were finished.

In her heart, she'd known they were not.

"I'm sorry," she said again in a more normal tone of voice, not sure how many times she'd already told him that.

"What happened?"

He was sitting on the floor, knees bent. She wasn't sure why he was down there like that.

"I—I just didn't feel good for a minute there," she said. Her face was tight, burning still.

"What's wrong? Do you hurt? Is it your stomach? Should we call the doctor?"

"No!" She needed to be left alone. "No, I'm better now," she said more calmly.

If nothing else, she had to keep Max from calling anyone. She couldn't go through the prodding, the questioning. And there was no reason for anyone to know. Her doctors in Austin had told her that. There'd be no physical harm from a panic attack. She knew what to do.

And how to prevent them.

"I'm concerned," he said, frowning. "Your health isn't something we want to mess around with."

"It was nothing, Max. Just something came over me for a minute there. It's happened before." She licked her lips, nervous as she treaded on unstable ground. "I just need a minute to let it settle and I'll be fine."

"You don't look fine."

"I'm tired. It's late."

He looked at his watch. "Nine o'clock isn't late."

Trying for a grin that she was afraid failed more than it succeeded, Rachel said, "It is when you're chasing around after a toddler all day."

"Talk to me, Rach."

Staring at him, Rachel searched for something she could say, something that would satisfy him, when she knew only the truth would do that.

And even if she could find a way to get the words out, she couldn't tell him now. Couldn't allow herself to trust him that much. Max didn't need her. Whenever their relationship reached the point where she was more trouble than pleasure, when the things he didn't like about her mounted up, he could just be gone. There was no need of her holding him there. Binding them together. Love, lust—they could bring a couple together. But it was mutual need that was going to keep them together until the end.

She realized now why, in spite of how much she loved him, she hadn't been able to tell him about her past all along.

The level of trust it would take simply wasn't there.

She couldn't tell him. He'd just try to help her, but this wasn't something he could find one of his answers for. There was no way he could erase the demons in her mind. No way he could go back two and a half years and undo the damage that had been done.

And no way that she could stand to be told what to do when she was already doing everything she could.

He joined her on the couch. Reached for her.

"Don't!" Rachel pulled back, her chest constricting again. Shaking, she slid farther away from him. "Don't." She hated the pleading tone, hated that she couldn't help herself.

His face froze and the warmth left his eyes.

"I'm sorry." This time the words were more a pleading for his understanding than an expression of sorrow.

She needed so desperately for him to leave her alone. To let it go.

Yet she knew that he couldn't. Part of her had known all along that it would come to this—the part that had made her run out on her own wedding. She was trapped. She had to tell him.

And she couldn't.

There was nowhere else to go.

"This has something to do with why you ran out on our wedding, doesn't it?" he asked, his voice as devoid of expression as his face. He was still sitting on the edge of the couch, only his arms had fallen from their outstretched position.

She nodded. Swallowed. *Please don't let him ask questions I can't answer. Don't make me hurt him any more than I already have.*

Rachel's mind reeled until panic almost set in again. Would the repercussions from that night so long ago never cease? Would they just continue assailing her until she was finally crushed?

So much for recovering and moving on. Getting on with her life.

What life? That of an emotionally crippled woman who could only be half-alive?

"Let me help you," Max said softly. His voice cracked on that last word, and Rachel's head shot up.

Something was going on with him, inside him. Something she'd never witnessed before.

"I'm okay, Max, really," she said. He was worried and he needn't be. At least not about her immediate condition. "I promise. If my health was in danger, I'd be the first to ask you to call for help."

She had Ruby to think about now.

Thinking of her little girl, sleeping so innocently upstairs, gave her strength. Even while the memories associated with Ruby's existence tortured her.

"You aren't going to marry me, are you?" Max's words quietly fell between them, turning her cold.

"Do you want to call the wedding off?" she asked. It's what she'd been expecting. She was too high maintenance now. She knew that.

It was going to take one crazy, needy man to put up with all her insecurities. Someone who needed her enough to have to put up with them.

"I want to help you, Rachel, to give you whatever you need. If you want me to be here, then I'm here. If not, I'll go. If you want to get married, we'll get married. If you don't, then we won't."

"What do *you* want, Max?"

"I told you." He rubbed his hands together, staring at them. "I want to help you."

Rachel shook her head, frustration giving her a measure of control. "I mean, for you," she said. "What do you want for you?"

He shook his head. "It doesn't matter what I—"

"I think it does." Where the firmness came from, she had no idea. But she stood behind it.

He was quiet for so long, she thought he was going to refuse to answer. He shook his head, squeezing his hands together. His shoulders slumped and his head bowed.

Not knowing what to do, Rachel sat there, trying to make herself as small as possible. She felt as if she were trespassing on his couch. He surely didn't want her there.

And she didn't blame him. During their entire relationship she'd been taking everything. Giving nothing.

Because he wouldn't allow her to give.

"Tell me, Max," she said, her voice barely a whisper. "What do you want? I have to know."

The truth would be better than the worry.

He turned his head, his eyes finally meeting hers, and Rachel gasped. There were tears in their black depths. And an emotional abyss she'd never expected existed.

He kept so much hidden, this man she'd been loving for most of her life.

"What do you want?" The words were torn from her, her heart fragmenting into pieces of pain. Hers. And now his.

"You." The word was husky. Broken. It was so unlike Max, Rachel was shocked. "All I want is you."

And then, before she could begin to assimilate what she'd just heard, Max stood, told her that he'd abide by whatever she decided, and quietly went upstairs.

She heard the door to his room shut with a soft click.

CHAPTER SIXTEEN

SHE HAD TO go to him. After sitting there, unmoving, for several minutes, Rachel was suddenly filled with an urgency she hadn't known in years. She had to go to Max. To comfort him.

And to find out if what she'd seen in his eyes was real. To know that she was really that important to him.

Important enough to risk telling him the truth.

Turning off the downstairs lights, making sure that the door was locked, she climbed the stairs as quietly as Max had.

His door wasn't locked. Turning the knob, Rachel pushed slowly, looking for Max in the gloom. He was lying on his back in the middle of the king-size bed, his feet crossed at the ankles, the back of one forearm covering his eyes. He still had his boots on.

"Max?" She called to him softly. This was his domain.

His arm came away immediately and he looked toward her in the light of the moon shining in through his uncurtained window.

"Something wrong?" he asked.

Rachel wanted to smile. And to cry. Still thinking of her. What he could do for her. Not even aware that she might be able to do something for him.

"Can we talk?"

"Sure." Swinging his legs to the floor, he rose, proffered the cushioned bench at the end of the bed.

Rachel sat on the bed instead. She patted it, inviting him to sit beside her. She didn't want to give him any ideas, pretend to promise anything she couldn't deliver, yet the intimacy seemed necessary.

"Talk to me, Max," she said.

"What about?"

"You."

"Me?" He turned his head and looked at her with surprise. "We know all about me," he said plainly. "It's you we aren't sure about."

Rachel shook her head. "What were you thinking about downstairs?"

"You."

She licked her bottom lip, wondering if she'd made a terrible blunder. Maybe there really wasn't more going on inside him. Maybe he'd just never learned to need anyone else. Maybe the damage his childhood had done, the lessons it had taught him were permanent.

Maybe he liked it that way.

"When you told me that you wanted...me...there was a look..." She stopped. She wasn't good at relationships. Not this kind. She had so little experience she felt like an idiot, sitting there, trying to help him when he probably didn't need her help at all. "What were you thinking about then?" she forced herself to finish.

"Nothing important."

"It's important to me."

He took a deep breath. Sighed. Tapped his hand against the side of his leg. "If you want to know the truth, I was handling a painful little bit of self-discovery," he eventually told her. "Rather uncomfortable for a man my age to be discovering things about himself that are contrary to what he's always believed.''

''What things?'' He sounded so vulnerable she wanted to touch him, but didn't dare.

''I've always been comfortable with my role in life.'' While it didn't sound like he was answering her question, Rachel was relieved that he was talking to her. ''I'm the caregiver, the go-to guy.''

She listened, nodding her head slowly, and waited for him to continue.

''I like being the go-to guy.''

Smiling at the almost childish belligerence in his very grown-up voice, Rachel said, ''I can tell. It's also something you're good at.''

''Thank you.''

''You're welcome.''

''So you can understand my unease when you came bursting back into my life, a beautiful young woman. After so many years of looking out for you—the kid with a giant crush on me—I suddenly found myself wanting to be more than just somebody who kept an eye on you.''

''What more?'' Rachel asked.

''I didn't know.'' He shook his head. ''And for a man who's used to having the answers, for others and for himself as well, it wasn't a comfortable place to be.''

She could see that. And though she wished she could rescue him from that uncomfortable place, she had a pretty strong feeling that he needed to be there if he was ever going to get the fullness out of life.

''I'm losing control, Rach.''

She frowned. ''Control of what?''

Standing, he moved over to the bench, pulled off his boots and his socks. Without a word, he left the room, and she heard water running in the bathroom. He came back minutes later with his shirt undone, rubbing a washcloth across his face.

"I'm losing control of the answers," he said, as though he'd never been gone.

"You don't know them anymore?"

"I don't *have* them anymore."

The distinction was apparently important.

"Who does?"

"I didn't know that, either," he said, tossing the washcloth on top of his dirty socks as he sat beside her again. "Until tonight."

She was afraid to ask. Afraid to hope.

"It wasn't until you asked me what I needed—and seemed desperate to know—that I asked myself. And I discovered who had the answers that had been eluding me all these months."

"Who?"

"You."

Joy flooded her so quickly she almost laughed out loud. But the confusion followed just as rapidly.

"I'm the last person with answers."

"Depends on the question," he said.

"So what's the question?"

"What's it going to take to make you put me out of my misery?"

She stopped.

His misery.

He'd told her more than once, jokingly, what misery he was in, waiting for their wedding night.

And they had been in the process of making love when the problems had started earlier that night. So this was about sex? Had that look been because she'd just led him on and then stopped before he'd had sex with her?

Nothing more?

"I don't know." She could barely hear her own words. She was right back where she'd started. With answers she couldn't share.

"I've never needed anyone before, Rach. Never had my own life subject to the whims of someone else. I've always been independent. And frankly, I'm much better at it that way."

She couldn't breathe, but in an entirely new way. An almost magical way. The seesawing of emotion was making her crazy.

"I didn't know what was happening, why I couldn't control the way I was feeling, the reactions I had to things that you said and did. I couldn't figure out why when you were in a good mood, I was, too. And when you weren't—"

"You need me," she whispered out loud.

"I sure as hell don't want to," he said, some of the masculine aggressiveness back. "I don't like it a bit."

"You wouldn't even let me wash your clothes."

"I'm a desperate man," he said with only half a chuckle, the underlying seriousness in his voice evident. "I think I've been maintaining what control I could in the name of making life easier for you."

"And making me feel pretty worthless to you in the process."

"Oh."

That one word said more to Rachel than months of conversation with him.

"You need me," she said again, the wonder of that

fact repeating itself over and over in the lonely and damaged depths of her heart.

"For my happiness," he said. "For the emotional stability I just always took for granted. You're in control now, Rach. It's not easy for me to say that, but I've always been a man who faces facts."

She knew that about him. Loved that about him.

"You need me."

He nodded. "You don't need to worry about it, though," he told her, sounding exactly like the Max she'd always known. "I'm a strong man. I've weathered many storms, and if you need to be free, I'm not going to do anything to stand in your way. It wouldn't be right for either one of us to keep you here if you don't belong."

He'd been able to keep up the bravado until the end. She heard the trace of fear, of anticipated pain in those last words.

"I belong," she said softly, taking a deep breath. "Max, I might be ready to tell you some things, but I need some promises first."

"You've got them."

Rachel stood, wringing her hands. "Hear them first."

Max leaned over and flipped on the lowest setting of his bedside lamp. She turned her face away.

"First one is, could you please turn that back off?"

He did so immediately.

"Second, you can't interrupt. I can't guarantee that I'll be able to get it out otherwise."

"Done."

"And third, please don't try to solve this one, Max, okay? Just listen."

His okay was a little longer in coming. But she had his promise.

She took a breath. And then another one. Concentrated on smooth, even, life-giving inhalations. And then, when she started to feel dizzy, she sat down on the bed, but not as close to him as she'd been.

"Tonight, when we—when you..."

"You don't want me," he said. "You don't have to explain or apologize."

"You said you wouldn't interrupt."

"Sorry."

"That's just it, I *do* want you, Max. At least, part of me does."

She couldn't go on. Couldn't do this. The words had been locked inside for so long that she just couldn't get them out.

Survival meant locking them away forever.

"What part of you doesn't?" Max asked softly after several minutes passed.

"The part that was raped."

In shock as she heard those words, Rachel burned all over. She sat there hoping she'd disappear. Waiting to disappear. There was simply no other option.

If it wasn't for the tension she could feel emanating from Max, the taut way he was holding his entire body, she might have believed she'd only thought those horrible five words. That their deafening reverberation was only in her mind.

"Say something," she whispered when she could.

"I think this is the part where you need me not to interrupt."

He sounded so normal. So real. So still there.

"It was my fault."

Nothing like getting it all out. When she'd tried to

imagine herself telling Max about that horrible time in her life, she'd always started from the beginning, telling the story in such a way that he'd know how it happened before he actually knew that it did. That he'd get the motivation first, and the facts when she'd laid enough groundwork for him to understand.

Both his hands were fisted on his thighs.

"I'd been drinking. I know I don't drink," she said quickly, before he could remind her of that fact. "It was the first and only time. It was stupid. And immature."

God, how she'd paid for that mistake. How she'd berated herself for doing something she'd known was wrong even while she'd done it.

But no amount of berating was ever enough. That mistake never lost its sting.

"I was at a party...." The words started to roll out too fast for her to choose them carefully. "My roommate had invited me. It was for her sorority. I didn't join one because I knew how much it was costing Daddy to have me at the U and so I loaded up on credit hours to get done in three years instead of four."

In the end, it had taken her four and a half years to get that degree.

"I don't know what happened to me," she said, still searching for the answer that had been eluding her ever since. "It was a Friday night, we'd just finished midterms, and when Melanie asked me to go with her, I said yes. I don't know who was more shocked, me or her, but I was bone tired. Tired of always doing what was right, of being the only one in the dorm on Friday nights, of never being able to join in the laughter with everyone else when they got back in at night and talked about the fun they'd had..."

The excuses sounded even weaker than they had the million times she'd repeated them silently in her mind.

"I can't justify the decision, Max. I went. It was wrong and stupid."

And she was still paying for that mistake. She wasn't ever going to stop paying.

True to his word, he didn't say anything. If Rachel had thought herself capable of interaction, she'd release him from his promise. She needed to know what he was thinking.

To get it over and done with.

"It turned out that the party was for couples. There was a guy there that I'd known from English class the previous semester. He'd asked Melanie to set us up. After years of being too busy with studies and church work to date, and being so in love with you—a man who'd never even given me a second look—it turned my head to have someone so interested in me.

"When he flirted with me, I flirted back. I thought it was harmless. Kids at a party. So many other people were around. I never dreamed..."

She stopped. Couldn't force another word past the constriction in her chest. Max now knew more than anyone else in the world about that night, her father included.

He still didn't say anything. Didn't release her. He was waiting for more.

"He offered to drive me home...."

She hadn't known she was going to cry. She'd thought she was numb. In shock. She'd only been worried about another panic attack.

"H-h-he sto-stopped..."

Tears streamed down Rachel's face, rolling past the

corners of her mouth. Their salt was all that was real to her.

"U-under a t-tree."

That tree. Oh, God. That tree.

"I fought him, Max," she said, embarrassed by how loud her voice was. "I kicked and tried to knee him, but he had me pinned on the seat. I scratched him, all the things we'd been taught in self-defense, but that only seemed to turn him on more."

That tree.

She couldn't tell him about that. Couldn't tell him why she didn't look at trees anymore.

"I couldn't even do the self-defense stuff right."

She'd hated to tell her father that. He'd been so insistent she take that class when it had been offered at the high school she'd commuted to in San Antonio.

"The whole time he was—was—was pumping into me, all I could do was stare at this tree hanging over the car." Tears dripped onto her hands. She left them there. "I just kept staring at the leaves, trying to make out shapes."

Other than clenching his hands on his thighs, Max hadn't moved. Hadn't said a word. Made a sound. She'd been wrong to ask for that promise from him. She now had no way of knowing if his silence spoke of disgust, of blame and disappointment, or at the very least, distaste. Or maybe he was merely honoring her promise.

She didn't know what else to say. She'd never gotten this far in the telling and had no idea how the scene was supposed to end.

And then Max sniffled.

And she realized that she wasn't the only one crying.

MURDER. Killing him as painfully, as brutally, as inhumanely as possible. Max could feel his fingers closing around a throat. His feet kicking a groin until it was no longer recognizable. Smashing a face. Breaking bones. Two-hundred and six of them.

He didn't care about the blood. Or the noise.

He cared about...

Oh, God.

He hadn't known he was crying. He couldn't ever remember feeling such helpless, devastating pain before.

His precious, sweet, intoxicating woman...

Murder. That was all he could think about.

Her hand, sliding over his thigh, seeking his own, brought him back from the brink of madness.

"Please say something."

Think. What did she need to hear? What could he possibly say to make this better?

And then he remembered that she'd asked him not to try.

Smart woman. She'd known...

"What happened afterward?"

He had some inexplicable urge to know the details. To experience them with her. So that she wasn't all alone in there, going through it by herself.

"He pushed me out of the car. Drove off."

Murder.

"We weren't far from my dorm. I righted my clothes as well as I could. I'd had a denim jumper on so no one could really tell..."

Max was afraid for a second there that he was going to lose his dinner. He needed to hold her, as though he could protect her. Yet he knew that was the last thing she needed.

"And when you got there?"

"I went straight to my dorm mother. Told her I'd been forced. We went to the hospital immediately and they did a D and C and called Daddy."

"So how'd Ruby…"

Max might not ever have had a sister, but he knew a lot about mating. And birthing.

Rachel sniffled. "No procedure is a hundred percent. At least one sperm had lodged itself somewhere where they didn't reach."

Castration. There was no other choice.

"Your father," he said, his voice sounding far off. "You said they called him."

"Yes. Daddy came immediately. He wanted to bring me home, but I couldn't bear to come back here and just sit. I was afraid that if I didn't get on with my life, I'd never have one. I had some crazy idea that if I pretended that nothing had happened, that everything was normal, it would be."

Max frowned. "But if your father was there…at the hospital…he knew about that night. Why didn't he know about Ruby?"

"Daddy and I stayed in a hotel in Austin for a couple of nights after the…incident. I didn't want to come home, but I wasn't ready to go back to the dorm.

"One night, when Daddy thought I was asleep, he kneeled to pray. I don't think he even knew he was talking out loud, but he was angrier than I'd ever heard, Max. Angry with the God he'd worshipped his entire life."

"That's understandable."

"It was frightening beyond belief," she told him. "*I* wasn't even angry and I was the one it had happened to.

"But when I found out I was pregnant, all that changed. I wasn't just angry with God, I lost all faith that He even existed. Hadn't I paid enough for the mistake I'd made? How could He let something so completely hideous happen to me?

"It was horrible, Max, losing the core upon which my entire existence had been built. I lost all sense of who I was. And if I reacted like that, how could I even hope that my father, with his anger already so strong, would be able to weather the news? I couldn't bear the thought of him losing his faith, too. He's a minister, Max. How could he be a minister without faith?

"And how could I possibly expect him to still love a God who would allow such a thing to happen to his only daughter?"

Max thought about that. He could see why she'd have reached that conclusion, especially in the state of mind she'd been in. He could even understand why Rachel would take such a drastic step as to hide her pregnancy from her father, deal with it all alone, in order to protect him. Rachel was a lot like him in that way—always serving others. With her, it came from a lifetime of living with a minister. Of giving service to those in need.

"He seems to be dealing with it all just fine," Max said after a couple of silent minutes.

"I know." She sounded amazed. And very very relieved. "Maybe because enough time has passed, and he sees that it all worked out."

Max didn't think so. "And maybe because your father knows far more about the God he worships than we do. Maybe his anger wasn't so much a crisis of faith as an honest conversation with God."

"Do you really think so?"

"Don't you?"

Rachel frowned, looking down at the floor. "I guess so," she said slowly.

Max had a feeling that Rachel's own loss of faith at such a critical time had come not just as a result of her pregnancy, but as a result of her father's reaction to the rape. That would have been a crisis in itself—for a minister's daughter to think that her father was turning his back on all that he'd believed in.

How could she have continued to have faith herself?

What a hell of a mess it had all been. A senseless, criminal mess.

And there wasn't a damn thing he could do about it.

"So, the bastard, he's in jail?"

"No." Rachel's voice was small. "I never told anyone...they just thought it was a stranger."

"The police weren't called?"

"Yeah." Rachel's fingers squeezed his, though he wasn't sure she knew. "I gave a description. They never found him."

So she could tell him who the bastard was. Max could find him. He was kind of glad the police hadn't gotten to him first.

"Why didn't you tell them, Rachel? The man deserves to pay for what he did to you."

"It would be my word against his," she said. "Date rape's not like regular rape, Max. Everyone at that party saw me flirting with him. They all knew I went with him willingly."

"You could—"

"No, Max, I couldn't. I couldn't go through that court battle, have my most private horror strewn around for strangers to deliberate, have my own morality questioned. Especially when I knew the fault was partly mine.''

"So we'll go get him now."

"No!" She let go of his hand. "You promised me you wouldn't try to solve this."

He had.

"It wouldn't be any different now, Max. Still his word against mine. And there's no real evidence to prove that I didn't have relations willingly. I've got Ruby to consider. I don't want her knowing that her biological father was a rapist. Please promise me you'll let this drop.''

He knew he was going to hate himself, but there was no way he could deny her anything. Especially not when her words made a good bit of sense.

"I promise."

"Thank you." Rachel fell against him, as though, now that the telling was through, she was too tired to hold herself upright.

Putting his arms around her, Max pulled her with him until he was leaning back against the pillows. She laid her head on his chest. Let him hold her.

And with that, Max was satisfied.

There was nothing he wanted more in life than to hold Rachel Blair, to have her trust him enough to curl up against him after having just relived an episode of such brutality.

Nothing he needed more.

There would be no murder for him.

CHAPTER SEVENTEEN

SHE WISHED she could sleep. She lay there warm and secure, curled up on Max's chest, concentrating on his steady, strong heartbeat beneath her cheek, the even breathing that was taking her slowly up and down with him. If only she could close her eyes and sleep.

But her mind was filled with images, with a confusing array of thoughts and worries. With questions.

"Can I talk now?" Max's voice was gentle against the silence in the darkened room. "Or was the vow of silence on this issue permanent?"

Even then he was able to bring a smile to her face. "It wasn't permanent."

"Then the first thing I have to say is I love you so incredibly much."

Rachel looked up at him. That wasn't what she'd expected at all.

"You do?"

Even now? With all the baggage?

"More than ever."

"You a masochist?"

"No, I'm a realist, Rach, and I know that life hands out crap sometimes. I also know that the true test of character is how we deal with that crap. You got help immediately, put yourself in counseling, made and stuck by some very hard decisions. You acted responsibly, even to the point of putting yourself through hell to make sure that your daughter had the best possible home and that your father's life—as he knew it—was protected. And when it was all falling apart on you, you went back to find yourself. You took charge of your life from the very beginning and did everything you could to stay in charge of it.''

His words were like a warm soothing bath, washing away years of grit.

"You make me sound a lot better than I am."

"What you are is blind. But we'll work on that.''

Though she had no idea what she had to smile about, Rachel grinned. "We will?"

"You can count on it."

He held her lightly, his hands still. Very slowly, her cramped muscles started to relax.

"The next reason I love you more is Ruby."

Frowning, she looked at the shadow of buttons on his shirt. "Why Ruby?" She hated herself for what she'd done to her daughter. Given away the first eighteen months of her life.

And from Max's point of view, Ruby meant an unexpected ready-made family thrust upon him in the form of another man's child.

"Because you loved that baby enough to take care of her in the only way you knew how at the time of her birth. With her conception still so painful in your mind, you knew you couldn't give her the love she deserved, so you went to painstaking efforts to find someone who could.

"And because now, when she needed you, you were willing to chuck everything to give that baby the home and love she deserves."

Rachel didn't recognize the woman he was describing as herself.

She remained silent, smelling the soap and fresh air scent that was Max, thinking about what he'd said. She'd never thought of her actions the way he was presenting them, and yet, she couldn't find the lie in his words. And if he was even a little bit right...

Was it possible that she could start to like herself again? That she wouldn't be spending the rest of her life with the self-loathing that had been her constant companion for more than two years?

"You aren't to blame."

Had he read her mind?

"In your recounting of that night, every step of the way, you were pointing out your mistakes. I never once heard you point out anyone else's."

She couldn't blame someone else for what she'd done. One of the first things her father had taught her was her own accountability, the fact that, good or bad, she was responsible for her actions.

"What about your roommate?" Max asked. "Surely, after living with you for months, she knew what type of person you were. And knew what kind of party she was taking you to."

"Well, yes, but—"

"And knowing that, she didn't protect you when she saw you were in over your head."

She couldn't have known. She'd disappeared shortly after they'd arrived.

"And the guy..."

Max's voice changed. Rachel wasn't aware her fingers were clutching his shirt until he released them, holding her hand.

"We're going to leave that alone because I know that that's what's best for you, babe, and we won't talk about it again if you don't want to, but this I have to say. The guy was completely one hundred percent to blame. There is no excuse—I don't care if you stripped naked and danced on his face—there is no excuse for a man to force a woman. Ever. Period.''

"I didn't strip naked." She was trying for lightness, but the words were so thin she failed miserably.

"I'm quite certain there was no face dancing, either."

"No."

"There was just a naive young woman who'd done something very normal. She experimented with her first taste of social drinking in an environment of her peers where she felt completely safe."

Safe. The word hadn't been in her vocabulary in a long time.

"It was my only taste of drinking of any kind."

"In all seriousness, Rach, I want your assurance that you'll work on not blaming yourself. Or get back into counseling. Because as far as I can see, the only permanent damage that will be done by all of this is what you're doing to yourself."

Whew. His words hit her hard.

And nothing had felt better in forever. He was giving her her freedom. All she had to do was be strong enough to take it. It wasn't going to happen overnight. She'd been through enough counseling to know that. But to think that it might happen at all—that she might, someday, be able to forgive herself...

"I promise that I'll put myself to the task and not give up until I succeed."

"That's my Rachel."

But was she?

"There's more lasting damage, Max, even if I don't blame myself entirely for what happened."

"Surely you don't mean Ruby."

"Of course not." Her smile, this time, came straight from the heart. "She's the incredible good that came from the bad." Even if she'd just in these last few days begun to realize that.

"Then what?"

"Tonight. My reaction. That's not just going to go away."

He said nothing and Rachel sat up. She wasn't sure she had the right to be lying all over him anymore.

"I can't help it, Max. I want you. I get, you know, that feeling. And then, without warning, I freak."

His eyes were piercing in the darkness, small white glints of strength and will. "Do you trust me, Rach?"

"Of course." She stared right back at him.

"I mean really trust me."

"With my life. And Ruby's."

"Then we'll get through this."

She wanted to believe him. But she couldn't see it. "How?"

"With time. And patience. With love. I've seen fillies who were beaten within minutes of their lives learn to take a rider again and be the best damn horses in the stable. All it takes is trust, babe. We'll build on what's there until one day, you'll be soaring in my arms, free from the demons."

Sure sounded like a pretty great story, if a bit of a fairy tale.

"We'll start out slow." His voice dropped, filled with sexy desire, and yet asking nothing. "We'll touch until you first begin to get tense. We won't let it get to the point where you panic."

How did he know her so well?

"Like this," he said, pulling her back against him,

slowly rubbing his hand up and down her back. He didn't take it any further. Just touched her. Innocuously, in a place where she'd find pleasure and no threat.

"And what if it takes a long time?" she had to ask. "That's not fair to you."

"Life's not fair, Rach, but if we endure to the end, the prize will be that much greater."

He made it all sound so…so…doable.

"I love you," she whispered. She had never meant the words more.

"And that's all I need."

She didn't know how that could be, but she knew that it was. Deep in her heart, she knew that Max was telling her the truth. Not only did he need her, but she was all that he needed.

Somehow, in a life that was broken and hopeless, a miracle had happened. She was finding the self she'd thought she'd lost, only she was better, stronger than she'd been before. And perhaps, regaining her faith as well.

With that thought, and a tiny smile on her lips, Rachel laid her head back down on Max's chest. And slept.

HATTIE DEVEREAUX walked slowly back to her own cabin. The slight young thing she'd just left in one of the smaller cabins she kept up on her property was due to give birth any day now. Hattie only hoped the Mexican girl made it through the ordeal. Right now little Juanita didn't look strong enough to make dinner, let alone push a child into the world.

For once, Hattie wished she had indoor plumbing in the spacious one-room cabin she called home these days. She'd love the decadence of a long hot shower pulsing down on her old bones. Somehow over the years of birthing babies for poor expectant mothers who had nowhere else to go, she'd grown a little rotund herself. The extra weight was hard to carry around.

Maybe the next time she bartered in exchange for payment for her services—payment she rarely received—she'd see about learning how to cook something a little healthier than her years in the Louisiana bayou had taught her.

Or maybe not. A bit of that chicken Creole she had in the icebox in her kitchen would surely taste dandy right now. It was Saturday. She could splurge on her noon meal.

Approaching her front door, visions of the dinner she'd be enjoying in a few short minutes dancing in her mind, Hattie didn't detect anything amiss until it was too late to conceal herself.

At the same time that she noticed the kicked-in front door, the broken lamp—a hand-painted beauty from one of her patients years back—the pickles lying limp in their own juice by the living room couch, the three men ripping into her couch with knives noticed her.

"Get her!"

When she heard the words, she turned and ran as fast as her tired old legs could manage. But it wasn't fast enough.

"I got nothing," she muttered as she landed, face-down, on the ground. "But you're welcome to whatever you find." She barely had the air to get the words out with the heavy brute sitting on top of her.

She wasn't going to fight them. She didn't have anything in that cabin worth fighting for.

"Where'd you hide it?" another of the men growled from somewhere above her.

Heart beating fast enough to be dangerous, Hattie tried to stay calm. She was used to taking care of herself.

"Hide what?" she gasped.

"The locket, damn you." The man on top of her punctuated his words with a knee in the middle of her back.

"I...don't...know...nothing...about...no...locket," she rasped, beginning to see stars.

Just when she thought she was going to pass out from lack of oxygen, the man on top of Hattie dragged her to her feet. The first thing she did was suck air into her lungs.

The second was get a good look at her attackers. Two were dark-haired. One blonde. All three were well over six feet tall and spent a lot of time working those muscles. They looked like somebody's henchmen.

"You get your old fat ass in that house and show us where you put the locket," the man holding her said. She walked as fast as she could, but it wasn't fast enough. The men took turns pushing her, hauling her back up when she fell.

The second time they mentioned the locket, Hattie knew who they were. Knew, too, that they were probably going to kill her.

She should be panicking. Begging. At least crying from the pain in her back and her skinned knees and hands.

Instead, all she could think of was steel. And that sweet woman, Julie Cooper. She'd been so generous to Hattie and her crusade all those months ago, writing such an incredibly touching story, she'd led many more women and babies to Hattie for help.

"Where is it, woman?" one of the men demanded roughly, shaking Hattie until she was dizzy as they stepped inside her mutilated cabin.

Seeing her few possessions demolished should hurt. But Hattie wasn't feeling any pain.

"I hocked it," she said, her voice as strong as her thoughts.

Sweet Julie Cooper, who'd been so broken the next time Hattie had seen her. Disillusioned, pregnant, on the run from a mobster husband. She'd stayed right there on Hattie's land, in one of the little cabins. And she'd given Hattie her locket as payment for the birthing of her son.

"Liar!" The blow to the side of her head caught Hattie by surprise. Everything went black for a quick second, and then she could see again.

She hadn't actually hocked the locket. But she *had* hocked the diamond in it to buy supplies for her babies.

"I needed the money," she said now, hoping she was instilling the right combination of begging and a refusal to be badgered at the same time.

Her head was aching. And she thought she felt blood dripping from her right ear.

Still there was no fear.

"Rip the place apart," someone yelled. "I'm giving you one more chance to tell us where you put that locket," the same voice growled just behind Hattie.

"I told you I hocked it." The dizziness was returning. She wasn't sure how long she was going to be able to stand there.

Someone needed to look in on Juanita later that night. Who was going to do that?

The second blow landed without Hattie seeing it coming. She heard a great roaring in her ears before she realized that she'd just been hit in the mouth. She tasted the blood before she felt the pain of broken teeth.

"Bitch," a voice hissed. Their voices all sounded the same to Hattie. Was there only one man there? Why had she thought there were three?

"Where'd you hock it?"

"Louisiana," she said, though she wasn't sure that was right. She'd hocked so many things...

He slapped her face, a ring or some other piece of metal cutting into her with a sting. She thought she could feel her flesh gaping.

But she was still standing.

Wasn't she?

It felt like she was. But was that the floor coming up so close?

Hattie landed with a thump against the hard wood of the cabin floor.

"Where in Louisiana?"

A face was pressing up to hers, the breath bad enough to choke her if she'd had the energy to choke.

"Louie's," she said. Short for Louisiana. It was all she could come up with.

Someone kicked her in the side and then in the stomach. Hattie coughed then, a trickle of warm liquid drooling out of her mouth.

She had a few minutes to herself after that. Minutes when she lay there in blessed peace, waiting for it all to end. She could hear them butchering everything she owned. Material ripping.

Her mattress, she thought. Or maybe a dress. The blue one. It had a hole in it and was a little small.

Glass broke. Things thudded as they hit walls and

floors. She couldn't really tell. Didn't think she cared all that much.

Something scraped. Like a knife on a wall.

One of her knives? Or theirs?

It was one of hers. A man hauled her up and over to her ripped-up couch, showing her the white stuffing that was bursting out all over the piece of furniture and beyond. "Tell us where you put that locket or I'll use this on you."

"Hocked it," Hattie said, cutting her tongue on a broken tooth.

The knife didn't really hurt when it slid into her neck, not like she'd have thought it would. Odd.

And the stuffing was soft as lamb's wool. She pressed her face in it when she fell. Soft and hers. She liked that.

In less than a minute, or maybe a lot longer, the men were gone. The cabin was blissfully, sweetly quiet.

She was going to lie right there and rest. She was so tired. Sleep was calling her, promising her sweet dreams.

But wait. She had something she had to do first.

With energy she dredged up with the love she had for Julie Cooper, Hattie rolled off the couch and, on her belly, pulled herself over to the phone. Once she got there, though, she couldn't make her arm lift high enough to get to the receiver. The arm must be broken, but she didn't know when that had happened.

Using her other arm, Hattie yanked on the phone cord underneath the table until the phone fell down beside her, the receiver rolling off the cradle. Leaving it there on the floor, she took several minutes to dial the number she knew by heart.

It got easier after that. She laid her head on the receiver and waited for Julie to answer.

"He found me," she said, the hoarse whisper coming as much through the slit in her throat as anywhere else. "They want the locket...Julie...the locket..."

There. She could rest now.

Her work was done.

WITH SHAKING HANDS, Rachel reached up to pin the lacy white veil around the complicated twist that was her long red hair.

Her wedding day.

She was going to do it. She was actually going to do it.

A knock sounded on the door, followed by, "Rach?"

It was Max.

Catching sight of herself in the mirror, a picture of the classic radiant bride in her white gown and veil, Rachel couldn't help the impetuous grin she gave her reflection.

"Yeah?" she called back.

"Can I come in?"

Not according to superstition. Not on her wedding day. But she and Max had their own rules.

"Of course."

He came in quickly, shut the door of the choir changing room behind him. "Ruby's a hit," Max said, coming up to her immediately.

He wrapped her in his arms, hugging her close, and let her go—just as he'd been doing every time he walked in a room since their talk the other night.

He'd spent hours with her in his room just kissing her. Touching her without holding her.

Exploring her boundaries.

Boundaries that were already changing.

Rachel reached up and kissed him fully on the mouth, needing a taste of his hunger.

"I love you," she whispered.

"I love you, too, babe. So much."

It wasn't the words that melted her, but the undeniable need she heard in his voice. A need he was no longer trying to hide from himself. Or from her.

He looked so incredibly handsome, standing there in a full tuxedo that was as black as his hair and eyes. So distinguished.

Without warning Rachel felt a flood of desire pool in her belly and lower.

"What?" he asked, staring at her, suddenly alert.

Embarrassed, not realizing that she'd given herself away by the shock in her eyes, Rachel looked down.

And saw the bulge beneath her bridegroom's fly.

More warmth below.

Looking up at Max with an unabashed grin on her face, she said, "You're turning me on."

He laughed out loud. "I intend to spend the rest of my life doing that," he told her.

For a split second Rachel feared the coming night. Feared the invitation she'd just given him.

And then she opened her eyes and saw the man standing in front of her. This was Max. He knew. And loved her anyway.

"About tonight…"

He cut her off with a gentle finger to her lips. And then a kiss where the only thing touching between them was their lips.

"We'll go just like every other night this week," he said softly when the kiss ended. "We'll explore. Together. You and me. And where the journey stops, it stops.''

Rachel frowned. She loved him too much to do that to him. He was a man who'd been waiting a very long time.

''But, Max,'' she said, carefully choosing her words. ''I can't keep doing this to you. I love you too much. Maybe if you just do it gently, and kind of quick...''

''You'll see me in hell first.'' There was no hint of a smile on his lips.

''But it might take months.''

''Then our first time will be so phenomenal it'll make history.''

''I can't do that to you.''

Didn't he get it? He was doing it again. Making it all about her. Not letting her take care of him.

He pondered her for a moment, and then the creases on his brow eased. ''If it gets to the point of painful, I'll teach you how to help me out in other ways.''

Rachel blushed from her toes to her scalp. All at once. The hottest flood of desire she'd ever known.

''Promise?'' she asked, not at all as coyly as she should have, given her lack of experience.

The thought of having Max completely at her mercy was heady. More of a turn on than the tux. She'd be in total control.

''I promise,'' he said, his eyes darkening as he watched the expressions flitting across her face.

''Tonight?''

''Lady, if you don't stop now, I won't make it until tonight.'' The growl was playful. And fully serious.

Rachel stopped.

But only because her father and Ashley descended on them to shoo them off down the aisle.

For better or worse, she was finally going to become Mrs. Max Santana.

DYLAN PULLED at the collar of his tux. For the second time in as many weeks he was all trussed up like a turkey at the market. Why couldn't folks just get married in blue jeans and oxfords?

It would sure as hell be a lot more fun...

His grumbling countenance disappeared when Rachel appeared at the end of the makeshift aisle on the lawn of her father's church.

She looked like an angel in her white dress and veil, more beautiful than he'd ever seen her. More than radiant, she was ethereal, alight with an otherworldly joy that he'd never seen before. One he was never going to forget.

Max tried to hide a cough beside him.

"You're a lucky son of a bitch," Dylan said under his breath.

"I know."

"You deserve her."

"I hope so."

"I know so."

The wedding march started. Rachel's step was sure, confident as she walked down the aisle on her father's arm. Her smile was unmistakable through the thin layer of veil across her face and her eyes were trained only on Max.

Dylan envied them so much it hurt. Life's trials would be bearable with someone who loved you so completely by your side.

Reverend Blair handed Rachel over to Max and took his place in front of them. The minister now, as well as father of the bride. He began the speech Dylan had been prepared to hear two weeks ago. But before he'd completed the first sentence, the emergency beeper Dylan always wore started to vibrate.

Stepping off behind Max, away from the view of the crowd, he lifted his jacket and read the scrolled message. It was marked urgent. Sebastian had found Hattie Devereaux. Julie was frantic with fright. He had to get help for Hattie. He had to go get Julie.

It was the call he'd been waiting for for months.

Glancing up from the beeper, he saw Max and Rachel, hands entwined, looking at him. They nodded in unison.

And Dylan, handing Max the ring he'd insisted on carrying this time, hurried down the side of the row of chairs that had been set up on the lawn, hardly seeing Ruby as she reached out to him from Debbie Anderson's lap. He only hoped he wasn't too late.

As he ran from the wedding, his mind's eye replayed the last glimpse he'd had of the bridal couple, and saw the angel his friend and surrogate older brother was in the process of marrying. The panic completely left his breast for a moment as he thought about Max kissing his bride.

There was some kind of powerful spell surrounding the people gathered at the First Trueblood Presbyterian Church that day. Something stronger than human will or good intentions. Something strong enough to carry mere mortals through the trials they would face. Something beautiful and eternal and safe. It came straight from Rachel. Enveloped Max and her baby. Her father. The town that she loved.

It enveloped Dylan, too.

And gave him hope.

TRUEBLOOD, TEXAS
continues next month with

DYLAN'S DESTINY
by
Kimberly Raye

Dylan Garrett would have done anything to keep Julie Cooper and her baby safe, but danger is closing in on them. He wants Julie to hide…to run away. But Julie wants the nightmare to end—now. She won't run anymore. This time, she'll stand side by side with Dylan and fight for what she loves….

Coming next month

Here's a preview!

CHAPTER ONE

HE WAS TOO LATE.
The thought hammered through Dylan Garrett's head as he slammed his foot down on the gas pedal. The Jeep Wrangler sucked gas and roared down the dark stretch of Interstate 10, gobbling up pavement the way his prized black lab, Dallas, ate up a convict's scent.

He couldn't be too late. He *wouldn't* be.

Dylan had spent the past ten years since he'd met Julie Matthews Cooper being too late. Time had beat him at every turn. He'd been too late to make an impression before his best friend won her heart. Too late to declare his feelings and beg her not to marry his friend. Too late to save her when that friend had turned from her husband into her enemy. Too late to help her through a difficult pregnancy spent alone and on the run.

No more.

The highway markers blurred past him as he drove faster, leaving the bright lights of San Antonio and heading north. His heart pounded as he descended the exit ramp and headed through the quiet Texas town. Quiet, as in calm, undisturbed, *safe.*

That's why he'd picked it as an ideal hiding place for Julie Cooper. His old college buddy. His dearest friend. The love of his life.

If only she knew.

The Jeep roared louder as he checked his mirrors before zooming through a red light. He'd been standing up as best man at Max and Rachel Santana's wedding when he'd received Julie's frantic call. Rushing off before the ceremony had barely begun, Dylan had foregone any timely apologies. If anyone would understand his quick disappearance, it was Max and Rachel. Their road to happiness had been rocky at best, after Max learned that Rachel had given up her baby daughter for adoption. Now the three of them were reunited, had worked through their differences, and the future looked bright, indeed.

Things were different for Dylan and Julie. There would be no happily ever after. No two-story house with a sprawling oak tree out front. No wraparound porch littered with toys and kids.

Forget day-to-day living with its ups and downs. Tears and laughter. Joys and sorrow. The future centered around survival, which is why Dylan had hauled ass out of the reception, much to his family's dismay.

But Boot Hill was a long drive from Trueblood, and Dylan prayed he would make it in time.